FUNNY AKADEMY

WOULD YOU RATHER BOOK FOR KIDS

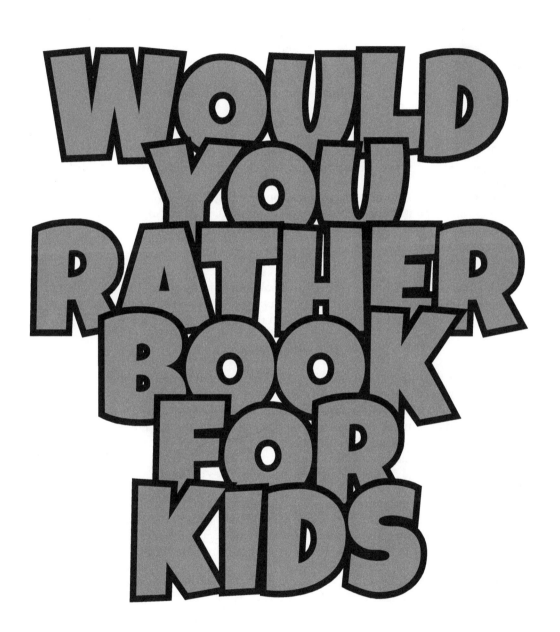

JIMMY ELLIOTT

TABLE OF CONTENTS

INTRODUCTION   4

WOULD YOU RATHER   6

RUNNY RIDDLES   106

INTRODUCTION

Would you rather is a conversation or party game that poses a dilemma in the form of a question beginning with "would you rather".

The dilemma can be between two supposedly good options such as "Would you rather have the power of flight or the power of invisibility?"

Two attractive choices such as "Would you rather have money or have fame?"

or two supposedly bad options such as "Would you rather sleep with your best friend's lover or your lover's best friend?".

The players, sometimes including the questioner, then must choose their answers.

Answering "neither" or "both" is against the rules.

This leads the players to debate their rationales.

Would you Rather...
drink sour milk
~ or ~
eat rotten eggs

Would you Rather...
drive a police car
~ or ~
an ambulance

Would you Rather...
eat a beetle
~ or ~
get stung by a bee

Would you Rather...
eat a bowl of spaghetti thatwas just one long noodle
~ or ~
eat ice cream launched from acatapult

Would you Rather...
eat a popsicle
~ or ~
a cupcake

Would you Rather...
eat a raw potato
~ or ~
a whole lime

Would you Rather...
eat a worm
~ or ~
a grasshopper

Would you Rather...
eat broccoli flavored icecream
~ or ~
meat flavored cookies

Would you Rather...
eat donuts
~ or ~
candy

Would you Rather...
eat your favorite food everyday
~ or ~
find 5 dollars under yourpillow every morning

Would you Rather...
every vegetable you eat tastelike candy but still be healthy
~ or ~
all water you drink taste like adifferent delicious beverageevery time you drink it

Would you Rather...
fly a kite
~ or ~
ride on a scooter

Would you Rather...
get a new pair of shoes
~ or ~
a jacket

Would you Rather...
get to name a newlydiscovered tree
~ or ~
a newly discovered spider

Would you Rather...
give up eating sweets
~ or ~
give up eating fast food

Would you Rather...
go on a rollercoaster
~ or ~
go sky diving

Would you Rather...
go on vacation to a newcountry every summervacation
~ or ~
get an extra three weeks ofsummer break

Would you Rather...
go skiing
~ or ~
go to a water park

Would you Rather...
go to the doctor for a shot
~ or ~
the dentist to get a cavityfilled

Would you Rather...
go to the movies
~ or ~
go to a waterpark

Would you Rather...
go water skiing
~ or ~
snow skiing

Would you Rather...
have 100$ now
~ or ~
1000$ in a year

Would you Rather...
have a 3d printer
~ or ~
the best phone on the market

Would you Rather...
have a bubble gun that shootsgiant 5-foot bubbles
~ or ~
a bathtub-sized pile of Legos

Would you Rather...
have a full suit of armor
~ or ~
a horse

Would you Rather...
have a hand twice as big
~ or ~
half as small

Would you Rather...
have a jetpack
~ or ~
a hoverboard that actuallyhovers (no wheels)

Would you Rather...
have a magic freezer thatalways has all your favorite icecream flavors
~ or ~
one that has a different icecream flavor every time youopen the door

Would you Rather...
have a new cool shirt in yourcloset every morning
~ or ~
a new pair of shoes once aweek

Would you Rather...
have a pet dinosaur of yourchoosing
~ or ~
a dragon the size of a dog

11

Would you Rather...
have a pet hamster
~ or ~
a pet cat

Would you Rather...
have a picnic in a park
~ or ~
on the beach

Would you Rather...
have a piggy bank thatdoubles any money you put init
~ or ~
find ten dollars under yourpillow every time you wake up

Would you Rather...
have a real triceratops
~ or ~
a robot triceratops

Would you Rather...
have a slide that goes fromyour home's roof to theground
~ or ~
be able to change and controlwhat color the lights are inyour home

Would you Rather...
have a special room you couldfill with as many bubbles asyou want, any-
time you want
~ or ~
have a slide that goes fromyour roof to the ground

Would you Rather...
have an amazing tree house
~ or ~
your whole yard be atrampoline

Would you Rather...
have an amazing tree housewith slides and three rooms
~ or ~
an amazing entertainmentsystem with a huge TV andevery game console

Would you Rather...
have an unlimited supply ofice cream
~ or ~
a popular ice cream flavornamed after you

Would you Rather...
have butterfly wings
~ or ~
a horse tail

Would you Rather...
have eyes that change colordepending on your mood
~ or ~
hair that changes colordepending on thetemperature

Would you Rather...
have french fries
~ or ~
chocolate cake

13

Would you Rather...
have no homework
~ or ~
no tests

Would you Rather...
have one eye in the middle ofyour head
~ or ~
two noses

Would you Rather...
have pancakes every day forbreakfast
~ or ~
pizza every day for dinner

Would you Rather...
have super strong arms
~ or ~
super strong legs

Would you Rather...
have the chance to design anew toy
~ or ~
direct a movie

Would you Rather...
have to wear a clown wig
~ or ~
a clown nose for the rest ofyour life

15

Would you Rather...
have your room redecoratedhowever you want
~ or ~
ten toys of your choice (canbe any price)

Would you Rather...
it be warm and raining
~ or ~
cold and snowing today

Would you Rather...
it be warm and raining
~ or ~
cold and snowing

Would you Rather...
learn to surf
~ or ~
learn to ride a skateboard

Would you Rather...
lick a dirty trash can
~ or ~
the bathroom floor

Would you Rather...
live in a castle
~ or ~
a spaceship traveling far fromearth

Would you Rather...
live in a house where all thewalls were made of glass
~ or ~
live in an underground house

Would you Rather...
live in a mansion in the city
~ or ~
on a farm with lots of animals

Would you Rather...
live in a place with a lot oftrees
~ or ~
live in a place near the ocean

Would you Rather...
live in the North Pole
~ or ~
the South Pole

Would you Rather...
live on a sailboat
~ or ~
in a cabin deep in the woods

Would you Rather...
live on the Moon
~ or ~
live on Mars

Would you Rather...
meet a superhero
~ or ~
a cartoon character

Would you Rather...
meet your favorite celebrity
~ or ~
be on a TV show

Would you Rather...
moo like a cow after everysentence
~ or ~
bark like a dog

Would you Rather...
never eat cheese again
~ or ~
never drink anything sweetagain

Would you Rather...
never have any homework
~ or ~
be paid 10$ per hour fordoing your homework

Would you Rather...
never have to take abath/shower but still alwayssmell nice
~ or ~
never have to get anothershot but still be healthy

Would you Rather...
only be able to walk on allfours
~ or ~
only be able to walk sidewayslike a crab

Would you Rather...
only be able to wear yourswimsuit for the rest of yourlife
~ or ~
only be able to wear pantsand a winter coat

Would you Rather...
open one 5$ present everyday
~ or ~
one big present that costsbetween 100$ to 300$ once amonth

Would you Rather...
own an old-timey pirate shipand crew
~ or ~
a private jet with a pilot andinfinite fuel

Would you Rather...
play hide and seek
~ or ~
dodgeball

Would you Rather...
play in a giant mud puddle
~ or ~
a pool

Would you Rather...
play paint ball
~ or ~
laser tag

Would you Rather...
play soccer
~ or ~
baseball

Would you Rather...
randomly turn into a frog for aday once a month
~ or ~
randomly turn into a bird for aday once every week

Would you Rather...
ride a bike
~ or ~
ride a kick scooter

Would you Rather...
ride a roller coaster
~ or ~
see a movie

Would you Rather...
ride a skateboard
~ or ~
a bike

Would you Rather...
sail a boat
~ or ~
ride in a hang glider

Would you Rather...
see a firework display
~ or ~
a circus performance

Would you Rather...
see a giant ant
~ or ~
a tiny giraffe

Would you Rather...
speak every language
~ or ~
play every instrument

Would you Rather...
spend the whole day in a hugegarden
~ or ~
spend the whole day in a largemuseum

Would you Rather...
sweat honey
~ or ~
always smell like a skunk

Would you Rather...
take a coding class
~ or ~
an art class

Would you Rather...
visit the international spacestation for a week
~ or ~
stay in an underwater hotelfor a week

Would you Rather...
watch a two-hour movie
~ or ~
watch two hours of shows

Would you Rather...
always be an hour later toeverywhere you go
~ or ~
an hour early to everywhereyou go

Would you Rather...
be a doctor
~ or ~
a teacher

Would you Rather...
be a ninja
~ or ~
be a spy

Would you Rather...
be able to read really fast
~ or ~
to understand what you readreally fast

Would you Rather...
be able to read the minds ofbabies
~ or ~
be able to communicate withbabies

Would you Rather...
be able to talk to animals
~ or ~
be able to be an animal ofyour choice

Would you Rather...
be an Internet sensation fromdoing somethingembarrassing
~ or ~
from doing something nerdy

Would you Rather...
be bald
~ or ~
have really long hair

Would you Rather...
be famous but ugly
~ or ~
be unknown and reallyattractive

Would you Rather...
be given apples to eat
~ or ~
be given vegetables to eat

Would you Rather...
be homeschooled
~ or ~
go to a regular school

Would you Rather...
be hungry all the time
~ or ~
be thirsty all the time

Would you Rather...
be in a house filled withmarshmallows
~ or ~
a house filled with candy

Would you Rather...
be in your favorite video game
~ or ~
be in your favorite cartoon

Would you Rather...
be licked all over by a straydog
~ or ~
be followed all around by astray dog

Would you Rather...
be pranked
~ or ~
be a well-known prankster

Would you Rather...
be Spiderman's sidekick
~ or ~
Superman's sidekick

Would you Rather...
be stuck in a room with aclown that's not funny
~ or ~
with a clown that's quiteannoying

Would you Rather...
be stuck with a crying baby forthe weekend
~ or ~
with a baby that likes to dragyour hair

Would you Rather...
be the last born
~ or ~
have a baby sister

Would you Rather...
be unable to celebrateHalloween
~ or ~
be unable to celebrateChristmas

Would you Rather...
become a dolphin
~ or ~
have a best friend who's adolphin

Would you Rather...
brush your teeth with ketchup
~ or ~
brush your teeth with hotsauce

Would you Rather...
clean up your bathroom
~ or ~
clean up your bedroom

Would you Rather...
crawl around all the time
~ or ~
hop around all the time

Would you Rather...
dance in front of your familymembers
~ or ~
dance before your friends

Would you Rather...
dance like a chicken in front ofyour friends
~ or ~
dance like a chicken on theinternet

Would you Rather...
drink hot chocolate
~ or ~
chocolate milk

Would you Rather...
drop your new phone downto the toilet
~ or ~
drop your charm braceletdown the sink

Would you Rather...
eat a piece of gum from thestreet
~ or ~
give your already chewed gumto someone else

Would you Rather...
eat bread with butter
~ or ~
with jam

Would you Rather...
eat fish that's half done
~ or ~
fish that's half burnt

Would you Rather...
eat from mom's plate
~ or ~
dad's plate

Would you Rather...
eat on the living room couch
~ or ~
eat in your bed

Would you Rather...
eat something really hot
~ or ~
eat something really cold

Would you Rather...
eat something that's peppery
~ or ~
eat something that's spicy

Would you Rather...
face your fears
~ or ~
forget you have fears

Would you Rather...
fall asleep in class
~ or ~
fall asleep on the bus

Would you Rather...
fart in an elevator on yourway to class
~ or ~
fart in class

Would you Rather...
find a turtle in your swimmingpool
~ or ~
find a goose in your swimmingpool

Would you Rather...
forget how to read
~ or ~
forget how to write

Would you Rather...
forget to take yourtoothbrush for a sleepover
~ or ~
forget to take your towel for asleepover

Would you Rather...
get a brain freeze every timeyou drank something cold
~ or ~
stop drinking anything coldaltogether

Would you Rather...
get a huge bowl of punch
~ or ~
get a huge bowl of ice-cream

Would you Rather...
get a toy boat
~ or ~
go see a real life ship

Would you Rather...
get into a fight with ducks
~ or ~
get chased by ducks

Would you Rather...
get lots of hugs
~ or ~
lots of cuddles

Would you Rather...
go camping
~ or ~
go fishing

Would you Rather...
go to a birthday party
~ or ~
plan a birthday party

Would you Rather...
go to a boarding school
~ or ~
go to a day school

Would you Rather...
go to a new school
~ or ~
move to a new house

Would you Rather...
go to bed early
~ or ~
wake up early

Would you Rather...
go to the library
~ or ~
have a library in your house

Would you Rather...
go to the moon
~ or ~
go to the bottom of the ocean

Would you Rather...
have a babysitter who's reallyold
~ or ~
a babysitter who's reallyyoung

Would you Rather...
have a bird make a nest inyour hair
~ or ~
a chicken lay eggs in your hair

Would you Rather...
have a flying carpet
~ or ~
a car that can driveunderwater

Would you Rather...
have a lot of superpowers forone week
~ or ~
just one superpower for amonth

Would you Rather...
have a massive zit
~ or ~
a zit that won't go away

Would you Rather...
have a rabbit's ears
~ or ~
a rabbit's teeth

Would you Rather...
have a robot friend
~ or ~
a robot that can do anythingyou ask

Would you Rather...
have a squeaky voice
~ or ~
a really loud voice

Would you Rather...
have a toy that walks
~ or ~
a toy that talks

Would you Rather...
have all the drinks you couldever want
~ or ~
all the junk food you couldever want

Would you Rather...
have all your shirts beoversized
~ or ~
be really tight

Would you Rather...
have all your teeth fall out
~ or ~
have only two teeth

Would you Rather...
have bright pink hair
~ or ~
bright brown hair

Would you Rather...
have embarrassing pictures ofyou posted online
~ or ~
sent to your crush

Would you Rather...
have green eyes
~ or ~
yellow eyes

Would you Rather...
have large feet
~ or ~
large hands

Would you Rather...
have multicolored hair
~ or ~
hair that tastes like candy

Would you Rather...
have no eyebrows
~ or ~
have pink eyebrows

Would you Rather...
have only one close friend
~ or ~
lots of friends you're not tooclose to

Would you Rather...
have only white clothes
~ or ~
only multicolored clothes

Would you Rather...
have really large feet
~ or ~
feet so small you have to shopfor shoes at the baby'sdepartment

Would you Rather...
have soda come out of yournose
~ or ~
come back out of your mouth

Would you Rather...
have something stuck in yourteeth and not know
~ or ~
have something dangling outof your nose and not know

Would you Rather...
have to dance every time youheard a song
~ or ~
sing every time you heard asong

Would you Rather...
have to stay up all night
~ or ~
sleep all day

Would you Rather...
have your friends come over
~ or ~
go outside and play with yourfriends

Would you Rather...
have your leg stuck in thetoilet bowl
~ or ~
have your hands stuck in thetoilet bowl

Would you Rather...
help set the table for dinner
~ or ~
help clear the table afterdinner

Would you Rather...
keep your money with Dad
~ or ~
Mom

Would you Rather...
kiss your Teddy bear beforesleeping
~ or ~
whisper to it all through thenight

Would you Rather...
listen to an audiobook
~ or ~
read a hardcover book

Would you Rather...
live in a cave alone
~ or ~
live in a cave with a friendlybear

Would you Rather...
live in a tree house
~ or ~
on a houseboat

Would you Rather...
live with grandma
~ or ~
live with your cousins

Would you Rather...
lose all your baby pictures
~ or ~
lose all the pictures from yourlast birthday

Would you Rather...
lose your favorite toy
~ or ~
lose all your savings

Would you Rather...
meet a fairy
~ or ~
meet a goddess

Would you Rather...
meet a friendly dinosaur
~ or ~
meet a friendly dragon

Would you Rather...
meet a friendly monster
~ or ~
a monster who's looking forfriends

Would you Rather...
meet your ancestors
~ or ~
meet your greatgrandchildren

Would you Rather...
meet your favorite celebrity
~ or ~
meet the president

Would you Rather...
never have to go to bed again
~ or ~
never have to wake up early

Would you Rather...
only be able to listen to musicfrom the 60's,
~ or ~
never be able to listen tomusic again

Would you Rather...
pee into your school bag
~ or ~
pee on yourself in public

Would you Rather...
pet a giraffe
~ or ~
pet a hippopotamus

Would you Rather...
poop in your pants whenscared
~ or ~
pee on yourself when scared

Would you Rather...
pop a balloon with somethingsharp
~ or ~
blow a balloon till it pops

Would you Rather...
put up Christmas decorations
~ or ~
help with the cooking

Would you Rather...
roll in mud
~ or ~
have mud splashed all overyou

Would you Rather...
roll off your bed
~ or ~
roll onto your teddy bear

Would you Rather...
scream while watching a scarymovie
~ or ~
pee in your pants whilewatching a scary movie

Would you Rather...
see a shooting star
~ or ~
see a rainbow

Would you Rather...
shower with cold water
~ or ~
with hot water

Would you Rather...
sing loudly in the shower
~ or ~
sing loudly while on the toiletseat

Would you Rather...
sleep beside a skunk
~ or ~
sleep beside a pig

Would you Rather...
sleep in your bed
~ or ~
sleep with your parents

Would you Rather...
slip on a banana peel
~ or ~
slip while trying to avoid abanana peel

41

Would you Rather...
stain your mouth with chickensauce and not know
~ or ~
stain your hands with chickensauce and not have anythingto clean it with

Would you Rather...
stroke a friendly lion that'sawake
~ or ~
stroke an unfriendly lion whileit's asleep

Would you Rather...
swim in ice-cold water
~ or ~
swim in a pool of hot water

Would you Rather...
throw up on your crush
~ or ~
throw up on your best friend

Would you Rather...
touch your poop
~ or ~
dog poop

Would you Rather...
trip and fall while runningaway from someone
~ or ~
trip and fall while runningtowards someone

Would you Rather...
wake up with wings
~ or ~
wake up with a tail

Would you Rather...
wake up with your grandma'sface
~ or ~
wake up with your grandpa'sface

Would you Rather...
walk around with soap in yourhair
~ or ~
with an unkempt hair

Would you Rather...
dance
~ or ~
draw

Would you Rather...
watch cartoons
~ or ~
dress up as cartoon characters

Would you Rather...
watch TV in bed alone
~ or ~
watch TV on the couch withyour family

Would you Rather...
wear pajamas to class
~ or ~
go to class in your underwear

Would you Rather...
wear ugly shoes
~ or ~
shoes that are much biggerthan your feet

Would you Rather...
wear wet underwear
~ or ~
dirty underwear

Would you Rather...
be a detective
~ or ~
a pilot

Would you Rather...
be a famous musician
~ or ~
a famous business owner

Would you Rather...
be able to change the color ofyour hair whenever you want
~ or ~
be able to change the lengthof your hair whenever youwant

Would you Rather...
be able to create a newholiday
~ or ~
create a new language

Would you Rather...
be able to find anything thatwas lost
~ or ~
every time you touchedsomeone they would beunable to lie

Would you Rather...
be able to play the piano
~ or ~
the guitar

Would you Rather...
be able to talk to animals
~ or ~
be able to fly

Would you Rather...
be an art teacher
~ or ~
a physical education teacher

Would you Rather...
be bulletproof
~ or ~
be able to survive falls fromany height

Would you Rather...
be the author of a popularbook
~ or ~
a musician in a band whoreleased a popular album

Would you Rather...
be the funniest person alive
~ or ~
the smartest person alive

Would you Rather...
be trapped in a room with afriendly tiger
~ or ~
with 10 bumblebees

Would you Rather...
drink orange juice
~ or ~
milk

Would you Rather...
drive go for a drive in aconvertible
~ or ~
a double decker bus

Would you Rather...
eat a turkey sandwich withvanilla ice cream inside
~ or ~
eat vanilla ice cream with bitsof turkey inside

Would you Rather...
eat pizza for every meal
~ or ~
ice cream for every meal

Would you Rather...
fly an airplane
~ or ~
drive a fire truck

Would you Rather...
get up early
~ or ~
stay up late

Would you Rather...
go to the doctor
~ or ~
the dentist

Would you Rather...
hang out for an hour with 10puppies
~ or ~
10 kittens

Would you Rather...
have 5 brothers
~ or ~
5 sisters

Would you Rather...
have a magic carpet that flies
~ or ~
your own personal robot

Would you Rather...
have a personal life-sizedrobot
~ or ~
a jetpack

Would you Rather...
have a pool
~ or ~
a trampoline

Would you Rather...
have a ten dollar bill
~ or ~
ten dollars in coins

Would you Rather...
have breakfast on the Eiffeltower
~ or ~
dinner in a castle

Would you Rather...
have fireworks go off everyevening for an hour
~ or ~
have Christmas three times ayear

Would you Rather...
have the chance to design anew toy
~ or ~
create a new TV show

Would you Rather...
have wings but you can't fly
~ or ~
have gills but you can't swimunderwater

Would you Rather...
instantly become a grown up
~ or ~
stay the age you are now foranother two years

Would you Rather...
live in a house shaped like acircle
~ or ~
a house shaped like a triangle

Would you Rather...
be able to create a newholiday
~ or ~
create a new sport

Would you Rather...
live where it is always darkoutside
~ or ~
always light outside

Would you Rather...
move to a different city
~ or ~
move to a different country

Would you Rather...
only be able to crawl on allfours
~ or ~
only be able to walkbackwards

Would you Rather...
only be able to whisper
~ or ~
have an incredibly loud voice

Would you Rather...
play soccer
~ or ~
baseball

Would you Rather...
read a book
~ or ~
read a magazine

Would you Rather...
ride a roller coaster
~ or ~
go down a giant water slide

Would you Rather...
sneeze uncontrollably for 15minutes once every day
~ or ~
sneeze once every 3 minutesof the day while you areawake

Would you Rather...
stay a kid until you turn 80
~ or ~
instantly turn 40

Would you Rather...
sweat honey
~ or ~
always smell like a skunk?

Would you Rather...
take a coding class
~ or ~
an art class?

Would you Rather...
visit the international spacestation for a week
~ or ~
stay in an underwater hotelfor a week?

Would you Rather...
watch a two-hour movie
~ or ~
watch two hours of shows?

Would you Rather...
always be an hour later toeverywhere you go
~ or ~
an hour early to everywhereyou go?

Would you Rather...
be a doctor
~ or ~
a teacher?

Would you Rather...
be a ninja
~ or ~
be a spy?

Would you Rather...
be able to read really fast
~ or ~
to understand what you readreally fast?

Would you Rather...
be able to read the minds ofbabies
~ or ~
be able to communicate withbabies?

Would you Rather...
be able to talk to animals
~ or ~
be able to be an animal ofyour choice?

Would you Rather...
be an Internet sensation fromdoing somethingembarrassing
~ or ~
from doing something nerdy?

Would you Rather...
be bald
~ or ~
have really long hair?

Would you Rather...
be famous but ugly
~ or ~
be unknown and reallyattractive?

Would you Rather...
be given apples to eat
~ or ~
be given vegetables to eat?

Would you Rather...
be homeschooled
~ or ~
go to a regular school?

Would you Rather...
be hungry all the time
~ or ~
be thirsty all the time?

Would you Rather...
be in a house filled withmarshmallows
~ or ~
a house filled with candy?

Would you Rather...
be in your favorite video game
~ or ~
be in your favorite cartoon?

Would you Rather...
be licked all over by a straydog
~ or ~
be followed all around by astray dog?

Would you Rather...
be pranked
~ or ~
be a well-known prankster?

Would you Rather...
be Spiderman's sidekick
~ or ~
Superman's sidekick?

Would you Rather...
be stuck in a room with aclown that's not funny
~ or ~
with a clown that's quiteannoying?

Would you Rather...
be stuck with a crying baby forthe weekend
~ or ~
with a baby that likes to dragyour hair?

Would you Rather...
be the last born
~ or ~
have a baby sister?

Would you Rather...
be unable to celebrateHalloween
~ or ~
be unable to celebrateChristmas?

Would you Rather...
become a dolphin
~ or ~
have a best friend who's adolphin?

Would you Rather...
brush your teeth with ketchup
~ or ~
brush your teeth with hotsauce?

Would you Rather...
clean up your bathroom
~ or ~
clean up your bedroom?

Would you Rather...
crawl around all the time
~ or ~
hop around all the time?

Would you Rather...
dance in front of your familymembers
~ or ~
dance before your friends?

Would you Rather...
dance like a chicken in front ofyour friends
~ or ~
dance like a chicken on theinternet?

Would you Rather...
drink hot chocolate
~ or ~
chocolate milk?

Would you Rather...
drop your new phone downto the toilet
~ or ~
drop your charm braceletdown the sink?

Would you Rather...
eat a piece of gum from thestreet
~ or ~
give your already chewed gumto someone else?

Would you Rather...
eat bread with butter
~ or ~
with jam?

Would you Rather...
eat fish that's half done
~ or ~
fish that's half burnt?

Would you Rather...
eat from mom's plate
~ or ~
dad's plate?

Would you Rather...
eat on the living room couch
~ or ~
eat in your bed?

Would you Rather...
eat something really hot
~ or ~
eat something really cold?

Would you Rather...
eat something that's peppery
~ or ~
eat something that's spicy?

Would you Rather...
face your fears
~ or ~
forget you have fears?

Would you Rather...
fall asleep in class
~ or ~
fall asleep on the bus?

Would you Rather...
fart in an elevator on yourway to class
~ or ~
fart in class?

Would you Rather...
find a turtle in your swimmingpool
~ or ~
find a goose in your swimmingpool?

Would you Rather...
forget how to read
~ or ~
forget how to write?

Would you Rather...
forget to take yourtoothbrush for a sleepover
~ or ~
forget to take your towel for asleepover?

Would you Rather...
get a brain freeze every timeyou drank something cold
~ or ~
stop drinking anything coldaltogether?

Would you Rather...
get a huge bowl of punch
~ or ~
get a huge bowl of ice-cream?

Would you Rather...
get a toy boat
~ or ~
go see a real life ship?

Would you Rather...
get into a fight with ducks
~ or ~
get chased by ducks?

Would you Rather...
get lots of hugs
~ or ~
lots of cuddles?

Would you Rather...
go camping
~ or ~
go fishing?

Would you Rather...
go to a birthday party
~ or ~
plan a birthday party?

Would you Rather...
go to a boarding school
~ or ~
go to a day school?

Would you Rather...
go to a new school
~ or ~
move to a new house?

Would you Rather...
go to bed early
~ or ~
wake up early?

Would you Rather...
go to the library
~ or ~
have a library in your house?

Would you Rather...
go to the moon
~ or ~
go to the bottom of the ocean?

Would you Rather...
have a babysitter who's reallyold
~ or ~
a babysitter who's reallyyoung?

Would you Rather...
have a bird make a nest inyour hair
~ or ~
a chicken lay eggs in your hair?

Would you Rather...
have a flying carpet
~ or ~
a car that can driveunderwater?

Would you Rather...
have a lot of superpowers forone week
~ or ~
just one superpower for amonth?

Would you Rather...
have a massive zit
~ or ~
a zit that won't go away?

Would you Rather...
have a rabbit's ears
~ or ~
a rabbit's teeth?

Would you Rather...
have a robot friend
~ or ~
a robot that can do anythingyou ask?

Would you Rather...
have a squeaky voice
~ or ~
a really loud voice?

Would you Rather...
have a toy that walks
~ or ~
a toy that talks?

Would you Rather...
have all the drinks you couldever want
~ or ~
all the junk food you couldever want?

Would you Rather...
have all your shirts beoversized
~ or ~
be really tight?

Would you Rather...
have all your teeth fall out
~ or ~
have only two teeth?

Would you Rather...
have bright pink hair
~ or ~
bright brown hair?

Would you Rather...
have embarrassing pictures ofyou posted online
~ or ~
sent to your crush?

Would you Rather...
have green eyes
~ or ~
yellow eyes?

Would you Rather...
have large feet
~ or ~
large hands?

Would you Rather...
have multicolored hair
~ or ~
hair that tastes like candy?

Would you Rather...
have no eyebrows
~ or ~
have pink eyebrows?

Would you Rather...
have only one close friend
~ or ~
lots of friends you're not tooclose to?

Would you Rather...
have only white clothes
~ or ~
only multicolored clothes?

Would you Rather...
have really large feet
~ or ~
feet so small you have to shopfor shoes at the baby'sdepartment?

Would you Rather...
have soda come out of yournose
~ or ~
come back out of your mouth?

Would you Rather...
have something stuck in yourteeth and not know
~ or ~
have something dangling outof your nose and not know?

Would you Rather...
have to dance every time youheard a song
~ or ~
sing every time you heard asong?

Would you Rather...
have to stay up all night
~ or ~
sleep all day?

Would you Rather...
have your friends come over
~ or ~
go outside and play with yourfriends?

Would you Rather...
have your leg stuck in thetoilet bowl
~ or ~
have your hands stuck in thetoilet bowl?

Would you Rather...
help set the table for dinner
~ or ~
help clear the table afterdinner?

Would you Rather...
keep your money with Dad
~ or ~
Mom?

Would you Rather...
kiss your Teddy bear beforesleeping
~ or ~
whisper to it all through thenight?

Would you Rather...
listen to an audiobook
~ or ~
read a hardcover book?

Would you Rather...
live in a cave alone
~ or ~
live in a cave with a friendlybear?

Would you Rather...
live in a tree house
~ or ~
on a houseboat?

Would you Rather...
live with grandma
~ or ~
live with your cousins?

Would you Rather...
lose all your baby pictures
~ or ~
lose all the pictures from yourlast birthday?

Would you Rather...
lose your favorite toy
~ or ~
lose all your savings?

Would you Rather...
meet a fairy
~ or ~
meet a goddess?

Would you Rather...
meet a friendly dinosaur
~ or ~
meet a friendly dragon?

Would you Rather...
meet a friendly monster
~ or ~
a monster who's looking forfriends?

Would you Rather...
meet your ancestors
~ or ~
meet your greatgrandchildren?

Would you Rather...
meet your favorite celebrity
~ or ~
meet the president?

Would you Rather...
never have to go to bed again
~ or ~
never have to wake up early?

Would you Rather...
only be able to listen to musicfrom the 60's,
~ or ~
never be able to listen tomusic again?

Would you Rather...
pee into your school bag
~ or ~
pee on yourself in public?

Would you Rather...
pet a giraffe
~ or ~
pet a hippopotamus?

Would you Rather...
poop in your pants whenscared
~ or ~
pee on yourself when scared?

Would you Rather...
pop a balloon with somethingsharp
~ or ~
blow a balloon till it pops?

Would you Rather...
put up Christmas decorations
~ or ~
help with the cooking?

69

Would you Rather...
roll in mud
~ or ~
have mud splashed all overyou?

Would you Rather...
roll off your bed
~ or ~
roll onto your teddy bear?

Would you Rather...
scream while watching a scarymovie
~ or ~
pee in your pants whilewatching a scary movie?

Would you Rather...
see a shooting star
~ or ~
see a rainbow?

Would you Rather...
shower with cold water
~ or ~
with hot water?

Would you Rather...
sing loudly in the shower
~ or ~
sing loudly while on the toiletseat?

Would you Rather...
sleep beside a skunk
~ or ~
sleep beside a pig?

Would you Rather...
sleep in your bed
~ or ~
sleep with your parents?

Would you Rather...
slip on a banana peel
~ or ~
slip while trying to avoid abanana peel?

Would you Rather...
stain your mouth with chickensauce and not know
~ or ~
stain your hands with chickensauce and not have anythingto clean it
with?

Would you Rather...
stroke a friendly lion that'sawake
~ or ~
stroke an unfriendly lion whileit's asleep?

Would you Rather...
swim in ice-cold water
~ or ~
swim in a pool of hot water?

Would you Rather...
throw up on your crush
~ or ~
throw up on your best friend?

Would you Rather...
touch your poop
~ or ~
dog poop?

Would you Rather...
trip and fall while runningaway from someone
~ or ~
trip and fall while runningtowards someone?

Would you Rather...
wake up with wings
~ or ~
wake up with a tail?

Would you Rather...
wake up with your grandma'sface
~ or ~
wake up with your grandpa'sface?

Would you Rather...
walk around with soap in yourhair
~ or ~
with an unkempt hair?

Would you Rather...
dance
~ or ~
draw?

Would you Rather...
watch cartoons
~ or ~
dress up as cartoon characters?

Would you Rather...
watch TV in bed alone
~ or ~
watch TV on the couch withyour family?

Would you Rather...
wear pajamas to class
~ or ~
go to class in your underwear?

Would you Rather...
wear ugly shoes
~ or ~
shoes that are much biggerthan your feet?

Would you Rather...
wear wet underwear
~ or ~
dirty underwear?

Would you Rather...
be a detective
~ or ~
a pilot?

Would you Rather...
be a famous musician
~ or ~
a famous business owner?

Would you Rather...
be able to change the color ofyour hair whenever you want
~ or ~
be able to change the lengthof your hair whenever youwant?

Would you Rather...
be able to create a newholiday
~ or ~
create a new language?

Would you Rather...
be able to find anything thatwas lost
~ or ~
every time you touchedsomeone they would beunable to lie?

Would you Rather...
be able to play the piano
~ or ~
the guitar?

Would you Rather...
be able to talk to animals
~ or ~
be able to fly?

Would you Rather...
be an art teacher
~ or ~
a physical education teacher?

Would you Rather...
be bulletproof
~ or ~
be able to survive falls fromany height?

Would you Rather...
be the author of a popularbook
~ or ~
a musician in a band whoreleased a popular album?

Would you Rather...
be the funniest person alive
~ or ~
the smartest person alive?

Would you Rather...
be trapped in a room with afriendly tiger
~ or ~
with 10 bumblebees?

Would you Rather...
drink orange juice
~ or ~
milk?

Would you Rather...
drive go for a drive in aconvertible
~ or ~
a double decker bus?

Would you Rather...
eat a turkey sandwich withvanilla ice cream inside
~ or ~
eat vanilla ice cream with bitsof turkey inside?

Would you Rather...
eat pizza for every meal
~ or ~
ice cream for every meal?

Would you Rather...
fly an airplane
~ or ~
drive a fire truck?

Would you Rather...
get up early
~ or ~
stay up late?

Would you Rather...
go to the doctor
~ or ~
the dentist?

Would you Rather...
hang out for an hour with 10puppies
~ or ~
10 kittens?

Would you Rather...
have 5 brothers
~ or ~
5 sisters?

Would you Rather...
have a magic carpet that flies
~ or ~
your own personal robot?

Would you Rather...
have a personal life-sizedrobot
~ or ~
a jetpack?

Would you Rather...
have a pool
~ or ~
a trampoline?

Would you Rather...
have a ten dollar bill
~ or ~
ten dollars in coins?

Would you Rather...
have breakfast on the Eiffeltower
~ or ~
dinner in a castle?

Would you Rather...
have fireworks go off everyevening for an hour
~ or ~
have Christmas three times ayear?

Would you Rather...
have the chance to design anew toy
~ or ~
create a new TV show?

Would you Rather...
have wings but you can't fly
~ or ~
have gills but you can't swimunderwater?

Would you Rather...
instantly become a grown up
~ or ~
stay the age you are now foranother two years?

Would you Rather...
live in a house shaped like acircle
~ or ~
a house shaped like a triangle?

Would you Rather...
be able to create a newholiday
~ or ~
create a new sport?

Would you Rather...
live where it is always darkoutside
~ or ~
always light outside?

Would you Rather...
move to a different city
~ or ~
move to a different country?

Would you Rather...
only be able to crawl on allfours
~ or ~
only be able to walkbackwards?

Would you Rather...
only be able to whisper
~ or ~
have an incredibly loud voice?

Would you Rather...
play soccer
~ or ~
baseball?

Would you Rather...
read a book
~ or ~
read a magazine?

Would you Rather...
ride a roller coaster
~ or ~
go down a giant water slide?

Would you Rather...
sneeze uncontrollably for 15minutes once every day
~ or ~
sneeze once every 3 minutesof the day while you areawake?

Would you Rather...
stay a kid until you turn 80
~ or ~
instantly turn 40?

Would you Rather...
work alone on a schoolproject
~ or ~
work with others on a schoolproject?

Would you Rather...
be able to draw
~ or ~
watch someone else draw?

Would you Rather...
be able to turn yourself into abutterfly
~ or ~
be able to turn yourself intoan eagle?

Would you Rather...
Are you ready for another journey in your imagination?Would you rather
be cold atnight
~ or ~
be hot at night?

Would you Rather...
be in a room that's really darkbut warm
~ or ~
a room that's really bright butcold?

Would you Rather...
be much taller
~ or ~
much shorter?

Would you Rather...
be really huge
~ or ~
be really strong?

Would you Rather...
be without a nose
~ or ~
be without ears?

Would you Rather...
choke on your spit whiletalking
~ or ~
spit in someone's face whiletalking?

Would you Rather...
dig through a dumpster
~ or ~
fall into a dumpster?

Would you Rather...
eat a year's worth of pizza inone night
~ or ~
never eat pizza again?

Would you Rather...
eat oatmeal
~ or ~
eat cereal?

Would you Rather...
eat something roasted
~ or ~
eat something fried?

Would you Rather...
find your favorite socks thatwent missing
~ or ~
get brand new socks?

Would you Rather...
forget your friend's birthday
~ or ~
have your friend forget yourbirthday?

Would you Rather...
get a free boat cruise
~ or ~
a free plane ticket?

Would you Rather...
go swimming
~ or ~
relax beside the pool?

Would you Rather...
go to a dance with someonewho has bad breathe
~ or ~
someone who has body odor?

Would you Rather...
go watch a circus show
~ or ~
be a part of a circus show?

Would you Rather...
have a jacuzzi
~ or ~
a pool?

Would you Rather...
have a really scary smile
~ or ~
have a really loud laugh?

Would you Rather...
have a stain on your outfit andnot notice
~ or ~
a hole in your outfit and notnotice?

Would you Rather...
have claws as hands
~ or ~
have a hook as a hand?

Would you Rather...
have gum stuck to the bottomof your shoe
~ or ~
tissue paper stuck to thebottom of your shoe?

Would you Rather...
have milkshakes
~ or ~
have a smoothie?

Would you Rather...
have smelly hair
~ or ~
badly trimmed hair?

Would you Rather...
have the zip of your jeans cut
~ or ~
the button on your jeans falloff?

Would you Rather...
have your mom embarrassyou at school
~ or ~
have your friend embarrassyou at school?

Would you Rather...
lick milk like a cat
~ or ~
lick yourself like a cat?

Would you Rather...
live in the sky permanently
~ or ~
live underwater permanently?

Would you Rather...
lose your favorite blanket
~ or ~
your favorite Teddy bear?

Would you Rather...
meet your favorite band
~ or ~
get five concert tickets forfree?

Would you Rather...
not be able to taste anything
~ or ~
not be able to smell anything?

Would you Rather...
pee in a bucket
~ or ~
pee in a cup?

Would you Rather...
roll down the stairs
~ or ~
hop down the stairs?

Would you Rather...
scratch your butt in public
~ or ~
scratch your armpit in public?

Would you Rather...
sing with a crooked voice infront of your schoolmates
~ or ~
sing in a crooked voice in frontof complete strangers?

Would you Rather...
sound like an old person
~ or ~
look like an old person?

Would you Rather...
take the stairs
~ or ~
take the elevator?

Would you Rather...
travel by road
~ or ~
travel by air?

Would you Rather...
watch a funny YouTube videoonline
~ or ~
watch a cartoon on TV?

Would you Rather...
wear a clown's costume
~ or ~
have your best friend wear aclown's costume?

Would you Rather...
wear trendy sneakers
~ or ~
wear cute shoes?

Would you Rather...
be a falcon
~ or ~
a dolphin?

Would you Rather...
be a master at origami
~ or ~
a master of sleight of handmagic?

Would you Rather...
be a unicorn
~ or ~
a pegasus?

Would you Rather...
be able to eat pancakes asmuch as you want without ithurting your
health
~ or ~
be able to eat as much baconas you want without it hurtingyour health?

Would you Rather...
be able to make plants growvery quickly
~ or ~
be able to make it rainwhenever you wanted?

Would you Rather...
be able to remembereverything in every book youread
~ or ~
remember every conversationyou have?

Would you Rather...
be amazing at drawing andpainting
~ or ~
be able to remembereverything you ever read?

Would you Rather...
be an incredibly fast swimmer
~ or ~
an incredibly fast runner?

Would you Rather...
be given every Lego set thatwas ever made
~ or ~
get every new Lego set thatcomes out for free?

Would you Rather...
be the fastest person in theworld
~ or ~
can freeze time?

Would you Rather...
be too hot
~ or ~
too cold?

Would you Rather...
constantly itch
~ or ~
always have a cough?

Would you Rather...
drive a race car
~ or ~
fly a helicopter?

Would you Rather...
eat a hamburger
~ or ~
a hot dog?

Would you Rather...
eat a whole raw onion
~ or ~
a whole lemon?

Would you Rather...
fly a helicopter
~ or ~
a commercial plane?

Would you Rather...
get every Lego set that comesout for free
~ or ~
every new video game systemthat comes out for free?

Would you Rather...
go camping
~ or ~
stay in a hotel room?

Would you Rather...
go to the zoo
~ or ~
an aquarium?

Would you Rather...
have 3 legs
~ or ~
3 arms?

Would you Rather...
have a cupcake
~ or ~
a piece of cake?

Would you Rather...
have a new silly hat appear inyour closet every morning
~ or ~
a new pair of shoes appear inyour closet once a week?

Would you Rather...
have a pet penguin
~ or ~
a pet Komodo dragon?

Would you Rather...
have a purple nose
~ or ~
green ears?

Would you Rather...
have an extra finger
~ or ~
an extra toe?

Would you Rather...
have everything you drawbecome real
~ or ~
become a superhero of yourchoice?

Would you Rather...
have lived in the 1870's
~ or ~
in the 1970's?

Would you Rather...
have the power to shrinkthings to half their size
~ or ~
the power to enlarge things totwice their size?

Would you Rather...
have your very own housenext to your parent's house
~ or ~
live with your parents in ahouse that's twice the size ofthe one you live in now?

Would you Rather...
lay in a bathtub filled withworms for 5 minutes
~ or ~
lay in a bathtub filled withbeetles that don't bite for 5minutes?

Would you Rather...
live in a place that is alwaysdusty
~ or ~
always humid?

Would you Rather...
live next to a theme park
~ or ~
next to a zoo?

Would you Rather...
live without music
~ or ~
without movies?

Would you Rather...
never have to sleep
~ or ~
never have to eat?

Would you Rather...
be able to read minds
~ or ~
see one day into the future?

Would you Rather...
own a mouse
~ or ~
a rat?

Would you Rather...
play the guitar
~ or ~
the piano?

Would you Rather...
ride a camel
~ or ~
ride a horse?

Would you Rather...
ride in a hang glider
~ or ~
skydive?

Would you Rather...
start a colony on anotherplanet
~ or ~
be the leader of a smallcountry on Earth?

Would you Rather...
visit every country in theWorld
~ or ~
be able to play any musicalinstrument?

Would you Rather...
a tooth fairy ran off with yourtooth and left nothing
~ or ~
left a golden tooth?

Would you Rather...
be able to spit out ice
~ or ~
spit out fire?

Would you Rather...
be bald
~ or ~
have hair that's almosttouching the floor?

Would you Rather...
be feared by all
~ or ~
be liked by all?

Would you Rather...
be known as a genius
~ or ~
be known for being funny?

Would you Rather...
be pranked with a fake rat
~ or ~
a fake bug?

Would you Rather...
be stuck on an island alone
~ or ~
be stuck with someone whowon't stop screaming?

Would you Rather...
build a snowman
~ or ~
build a sand castle?

Would you Rather...
dance around the house inyour underwear
~ or ~
dance around theneighborhood barefooted?

Would you Rather...
do hand-painting
~ or ~
paint with a brush?

Would you Rather...
eat food out of the trashcan
~ or ~
not get any food to eat for anentire weekend?

Would you Rather...
eat only donuts for an entireweek
~ or ~
never get to eat donuts forthe rest of your life?

Would you Rather...
eat your favorite meal
~ or ~
eat a meal you've never hadbefore?

Would you Rather...
forget the way to school
~ or ~
forget the way to your class?

Would you Rather...
get a cat
~ or ~
get a dog?

Would you Rather...
get good grades
~ or ~
be really good at a sport?

Would you Rather...
go to a clothing store
~ or ~
go to a toy store?

Would you Rather...
go to summer school
~ or ~
summer camp?

Would you Rather...
have a baby throw up on you
~ or ~
a baby pee on you?

Would you Rather...
have a nose as long asPinocchio's
~ or ~
no nose at all?

Would you Rather...
have a sore throat
~ or ~
a cough?

Would you Rather...
have a unicorn of your own
~ or ~
be a unicorn?

Would you Rather...
have food spilled all over yourfavorite outfit
~ or ~
have a drink spilled all overyour favorite outfit?

Would you Rather...
have milk run down your noseevery time you laugh
~ or ~
have milk run out of your eyesevery time you cried?

Would you Rather...
have one leg shorter than theother
~ or ~
two really short legs?this book is full of cool and fun games, flip the page
Are you ready for another journey in your imagination?

Would you Rather...
always be dressed up
~ or ~
always wear your pajamas?

Would you Rather...
be a cyborg
~ or ~
a robot?

Would you Rather...
be a doctor
~ or ~
a scientist?

Would you Rather...
be a famous inventor
~ or ~
a famous writer?

Would you Rather...
be a master at drawing
~ or ~
be an amazing singer?

Would you Rather...
be a master at painting
~ or ~
an amazing dancer?

Would you Rather...
be a police officer
~ or ~
a doctor?

Would you Rather...
be a wizard
~ or ~
a superhero?

Would you Rather...
be able to change color tocamouflage yourself
~ or ~
grow fifteen feet taller andshrink back down wheneveryou wanted?

Would you Rather...
be able to change the color ofanything with just a thought
~ or ~
know every language that hasever been spoken on Earth?

Would you Rather...
be able to do flips andbackflips
~ or ~
break dance?

Would you Rather...
be able to eat any spicy foodwithout a problem
~ or ~
never be bitten by anothermosquito?

Would you Rather...
be able to fly
~ or ~
be invisible?

Would you Rather...
be able to learn everything ina book by putting it underyour pillow while you slept
~ or ~
be able to control yourdreams every night?

Would you Rather...
be able to move silently
~ or ~
have an incredibly loud andscary voice?

Would you Rather...
be able to move wires aroundwith your mind
~ or ~
be able to turn any carpetedfloor into a six-foot deep poolof water?

Would you Rather...
be able to remembereverything you've ever seen
~ or ~
be able to perfectly imitateany voice you heard?

Would you Rather...
be able to see things that arevery far away, like binoculars
~ or ~
be able to see things veryclose up, like a microscope?

Would you Rather...
be able to shrink down to thesize of an ant any time youwanted to
~ or ~
be able to grow to the size ofa two-story building anytimeyou wanted to?

Would you Rather...
be able to type faster thananyone
~ or ~
speak faster than anyone?

Would you Rather...
be able to type/text very fast
~ or ~
be able to read really quickly?

Would you Rather...
be an actor/actress in a movie
~ or ~
write a movie script thatwould be made into a movie?

Would you Rather...
be an athlete in the SummerOlympics
~ or ~
the Winter Olympics?

Would you Rather...
be an Olympic athlete
~ or ~
the President?

Would you Rather...
be fluent in 10 languages
~ or ~
be able to code in 10 differentprogramming languages?

Would you Rather...
be incredibly luck withaverage intelligence
~ or ~
incredibly smart with averageluck?

Would you Rather...
be invisible
~ or ~
be able to fly?

Would you Rather...
be really fast
~ or ~
really strong?

Would you Rather...
be ten years older
~ or ~
four years younger?

Would you Rather...
be the fastest kid at yourschool
~ or ~
the smartest kid at yourschool?

Would you Rather...
be the fastest swimmer onearth
~ or ~
the third fastest runner onearth?

Would you Rather...
be the worst player on a teamthat always wins
~ or ~
the best player on a team thatalways loses?

Would you Rather...
be unable to control how fastyou talk
~ or ~
unable to control how loudyou talk?

Would you Rather...
be wildly popular on the socialmedia platform of your choice
~ or ~
have an extremely popularpodcast?

Would you Rather...
control the outcome of anycoin flip
~ or ~
be unbeatable at rock, paper,scissors?

FUNNY AKADEMY

RIDDLE BOOK FOR KIDS

JIMMY ELLIOTT

INTRODUCTION

Riddles are a fantastic way to share quality time with you kids. It comes with several social and emotional benefits that can help improve the general performance of your kids. So if you haven't started sharing riddle time with them, now is the time to introduce it to them. This book is written with such philosophy as to helping your ward learn new things and stretch their mind. Here are a few ways to achieve this?

COPING SKILLS

Riddles will help your kids learn new coping skills and relieve stress better. They can adapt new mind blowing skills to get tougher at challenges in school and relating of peers. This book also has a lot of funny jokes that can ensure this coping is complete and thorough.

VERBAL SKILLS

Riddles will equip your kids with new vocabulary for communication. This will also aid for spelling and other terminologies that they need to excel in school.

ENCOURAGE FAMILY TIME

Riddles will help you spend quality time with your kids. This book will help you spend such quality time with your kids especially riddles that are funny and would want to encourage sharing between siblings.

In all Difficult Riddles For Smart Kids is prepared to be of massive benefit to you and your family. Prepare your mind for the wonderful times ahead.

Question:

With thieves I consort, With the Vilest, in short, I'm quite at ease in depravity, Yet all divines use me, And savants can't lose me, For I am the century of gravity.

Answer:

V

Question:

I move without wings, Between silken string, I leave as you find, My substance behind.

Answer:

Spider

Question:

What flies forever, Rests never?

Answer:

Wind

Question:

What type of cheese is made backwards?

Answer:

Edam

Question:

I appear in the morning. But am always there. You can never see me. Though I am everywhere. By night I am gone, though I sometimes never was. Nothing can defeat me. But I am easily gone.

Answer:

Sunlight

Question:
I crawl on the earth. And rise on a pillar.
Answer:
Shadow

Question:
They are many and one, they wave and they drum, Used to cover a state, they go with you everywhere.
Answer:
Hands

Question:
What must be in the oven yet cannot be baked? Grows in the heat yet shuns the light of day? What sinks in water but rises with air? Looks like skin but is fine as hair?
Answer:
Yeast

Question:
I have holes on the top and bottom. I have holes on my left and on my right. And I have holes in the middle, Yet I still hold water.
Answer:
Sponge

Question:
What can be swallowed, But can also swallow you?
Answer:
Pride

Question:

You get many of me, but never enough. After the last one, your life soon will snuff. You may have one of me but one day a year, When the last one is gone, your life disappears.

Answer:
Birthday

Question:
I run around the city, but I never move.

Answer:
Wall

Question:
As a whole, I am both safe and secure. Behead me, I become a place of meeting. Behead me again, I am the partner of ready. Restore me, I become the domain of beasts.

Answer:
Stable

Question:
Two horses, swiftest traveling, harnessed in a pair, and grazing ever in places. Distant from them.

Answer:
Eyes

Question:
At the sound of me, men may dream. Or stamp their feet. At the sound of me, women may laugh. Or sometimes weep.

Answer:
Music

Question:

To unravel me you need a simple key, no key that was made by lock-smith's hand. But a key that only I will understand.

Answer:

Riddle

Question:

Long and think, red within, with a nail at the end.

Answer:

Finger

Question:

I'm sometimes white and always wrong. I can break a heart and hurt the strong. I can build love or tear it down. I can make a smile or bring a frown.

Answer:

Lie

Question:

You can tumble in it, roll in it, burn it, animal eat it. Used to cover floors, still used beyond stall doors. Freshens whatever it is placed on. Absorbs whatever is poured into it.

Answer:

Hay

Question:

I come in winter. I cannot see, hear, or feel. I can't eat, But you can eat parts of me.

Answer:

Snowman

Question:

Sometimes I am loud. And viewed with distaste. Poke out my "eye", then I'm on the front of your face.

Answer:

Noise

Question:

What is it that has four legs, one head, and a foot?

Answer:

Bed

Question:

What makes a loud noise when changing its jacket. Becomes larger but weighs less?

Answer:

Popcorn

Question:

I am always hungry, I must always be fed. The finger I lick will soon turn red.

Answer:

Fire

Question:

Something wholly unreal, yet seems real to I. Think my friend, tell me where does it lie?

Answer:

Mind

Question:

115 No matter how little or how much you use me, you change me every month.
Answer:
Calendar

Question:
What can burn the eyes, sting the mouth, yet be consumed?
Answer:
Salt

Question:
What an fill a room but takes up no space?
Answer:
Light

Question:
It occurs once in every minute. Twice in every moment and yet never in one hundred thousand years.
Answer:
M

Question:
With pointed fangs it sits in wait. With piercing force it doles out fate, over bloodless victims proclaiming its might. Eternally joining in a single bite.
Answer:
Stapler

Question:
It holds most knowledge that has ever been said. But is not the brain, is

not the head. To feathers and their masters, it's both bane and boon One empty, and one full.
Answer:
Paper

Question:
Upon me you can tread, though softly under cover. And I will take you places, that you have yet to discover. I'm high, and I'm low, though flat in the middle. And though a joy to the children, adults think of me little.
Answer:
Stairs

Question:
A mile from end to end, yet as close to as a friend. A precious commodity, freely given. Seen on the dead and on the living. Found on the rich, poor, short and tall. But shared among children most of all.
Answer:
Smile

Question:
I have a hundred legs, but cannot stand. I have a long neck, but no head. I cannot see. I'm neat and tidy as can be.
Answer:
Broom

Question:
Flat as a leaf, round as a ring. Has two eyes, can't see a thing.
Answer:
Button

117

Question:
I don't think or eat or slumber. Or move around or fear thunder. Just like you I look the same but I can't harm you or be your bane.
Answer:
Doll

Question:
In marble halls as white as milk, lined with a skin as soft as silk. Within a fountain crystal-clear. A golden apple doth appear. No doors there are to this stronghold, yet thieves break in and steal the gold.
Answer:
Egg

Question:
What is it that you must give before you can keep it.
Answer:
Word

Question:
I dig out tiny caves and store gold and silver in them. I also build bridges of silver and make crowns of gold. They are the smallest you could imagine. Sooner or later everybody needs my help. Yet many people are afraid to let me help them.
Answer:
Dentist

Question:
What is long and slim, works in light. Has but one eye, and an awful bite?
Answer:
Needle

119

Question:
What lies in a tunnel of darkness. That can only attack when pulled back?
Answer:
Bullet

Question:
What has six faces and twenty-one eyes?
Answer:
Die

Question:
Until I am measured. I am not known, yet how you miss me when I have flown.
Answer:
Time

Question:
Three lives have I. Gentle enough to soothe the skin. Light enough to caress the sky. Hard enough to crack rocks.
Answer:
Water

Question:
I wear a red robe, with staff in hand, and a stone in my throat.
Answer:
Cherry

Question:
A warrior amongst the flowers, he bears a thrusting sword. He uses it whenever he must, to defend his golden hoard.

Answer:
Bee

Question:
I hide but my head is outside.
Answer:
Nail

Question:
A house full, a yard full, a chimney full, no one can get a spoonful.
Answer:
Smoke

Question:
You can spin, wheel and twist. But this thing can turn without moving.
Answer:
Milk

Question:
Halo of water, tongue of wood. Skin of stone, long I've stood. My fingers short reach to the sky. Inside my heart men live and die.
Answer:
Castle

Question:
When they are caught, they are thrown away. When they escape, you itch all day.
Answer:
Fleas

121

Question:
What does man love more than life, fear more than death or mortal strife. What the poor have, the rich require, and what contented men desire. What the miser spends, and the spendthrift saves. And all men carry to their graves.
Answer:
Nothing

Question:
In we go, out we go. All around and in a row. Always, always steady flow. When we'll stop, you'll never known. In we go, out we go.
Answer:
Tides

Question:
A cloud was my mother, the wind is my father. My son is the cool stream, and my daughter is the fruit of the land. A rainbow is my bed, the earth my final resting place. And I'm the torment of man.
Answer:
Rain

Question:
Born of earth, but with none of its strength. Molded by flame, but with none of its power. Shaped
Answer:
Glass

Question:
Remove the outside. Cook the inside. Eat the outside. Throw away the inside.
Answer:

Question:
This is in a realm of true and in a realm false, but you experience me as you turn and toss.
Answer:
Dream

Question:
There is an ancient invention. Still used in some parts of the world today. That allows people to see through walls.
Answer:
Window

Question:
Some live in me, some live on. And some shave me to stride upon. I rarely leave my native land. Until my death I always stand. High and low I may be found. Both above and below ground.
Answer:
Tree

Question:
Metal or bone I may be, many teeth I have and always bared. Yet my bite harms no one. And ladies delight in my touch.
Answer:
Comb

Question:
I am a fire's best friend. When fat, my body fills with wind. When pushed to thin, through my nose I blow. Then you can watch the embers glow.

Answer:
Bellows

Question:
Every dawn begins with me. At dusk I'll be the first you see, and daybreak couldn't come without. What midday centers all about. Daises grow from me, I'm told. And when I come, I end all code, but in the sun I won't be found. Yet still, each day I'll be around.
Answer:
D

Question:
You heart it speak, for it has a hard tongue. But it cannot breathe, for it has not a lung.
Answer:
Bell

Question:
I cut through evil like a double edged sword, and chaos flees at my approach. Balance I single-handedly upraise, through battles fought with heart and mind, instead of with my gaze.
Answer:
Justice

Question:
The eight of us move forth and back. To protect our king from the foes attack.
Answer:
Pawns

Question:
He has one and a person has two. A citizen has three. And a human being has four. A personality has five. And an inhabitant of earth has six.
Answer:
Syllable

Question:
If you break me, I do not stop working. If you touch me, I may be snared. If you lose me, nothing will matter.
Answer:
Heart

Question:
What's in the middle of nowhere?
Answer:
H

Question:
What force and strength cannot get through. I, with a gentle touch, can do. Many in the street would stand. Were I not a friend at hand.
Answer:
Key

Question:
Often held but never touched. Always wet but never rusts. Often bits but seldom bit. To use it well you must have wit.
Answer:
Tongue

Question:

125 As round as an apple. As deep as a cup. All the king's horses can't pull it up.
Answer:
Well

Question:
He stands beside the road. In a purple cap at tattered green cloak. Those who touch him, curse him.
Answer:
Thistle

Question:
Power enough to smash ships and crush roofs. Yet it still must fear the sun.
Answer:
Ice

Question:
What surrounds the world, yet dwells within a thimble?
Answer:
Space

Question:
I cannot be other than what I am, until the man who made me dies. Power and glory will fall to me finally. Only when he last closes his eyes.
Answer:
Prince

Question:
What is it that makes tears without sorrow. And takes its journey to heaven?

Answer:
Smoke

Question:
Inside a great blue castle lives a shy young maid. She blushes in the morning and comes not out at night.
Answer:
Sun

Question:
This thing runs but cannot walk, sometimes sings but never talks. Lacks arms, has hands; lacks a head but has a face.
Answer:
Clock

Question:
A word I know, six letters it contains. Subtract just one and twelve remains.
Answer:
Dozens

Question:
I go in hard and dry. I come out soft and sticky. You can blow me.
Answer:
Gum

Question:
I am the yellow hem of the sea's blue skirt.
Answer:
Beach

Question:

A skin have I, more eyes than one. I can be very nice when I am done.

Answer:

Potato

Question:

I have four legs but no tail. Usually I am heard only at night.

Answer:

Frog

Question:

A tiny bead, like fragile glass, strung along a cord of grass.

Answer:

Dew

Question:

Break it and it is better, immediately set and harder to break again.

Answer:

Record

Question:

Each morning I appear to lie at your feet, all day I follow no matter how fast you run. Yet I nearly perish in the midday sun.

Answer:

Shadow

Question:

What is it which builds things up? Lays mountains low? Dries up lakes, and makes things grow? Cares not a whim about your passing? And is like few other things, because it is everlasting?

Answer:

Time

Question:

I am the fountain from which no one can drink. For many I am considered a necessary link. Like gold to all I am sought for, but my continued death brings wealth for all to want more.

Answer:

Oil

Question:

Sleeping during the day, I hide away. Watchful through the night, I open at dawn's light. But only for the briefest time, do I shine. And then I hide away. And sleep through the day.

Answer:

Sunrise

Question:

A seed am I, three letters make my name. Take away two and I still sound the same.

Answer:

Pea

Question:

In the middle of night, I surround the gong. In the middle of sight, I end the song.

Answer:

G

Question:

129 Look into my face and I'm everybody. Scratch my back and I'm nobody.
Answer:
Mirror

Question:
Two brothers we are, great burdens we bear. All day we are bitterly pressed. Yet this I will say, we are full all the day, and empty when go to rest.
Answer:
Boots

Question:
They can be harbored, but few hold water. You can nurse them, but only by holding them against someone else. You can carry them, but not with your arms. You can bury them, but not in the earth.
Answer:
Grudge

Question:
What is it that was given to you, belongs only to you. And yet your friends use it more than you do?
Answer:
Name

Question:
By Moon or by Sun, I shall be found. Yet I am undone, if there's no light around.
Answer:
Shadow

Question:

What do you use to hoe a row, slay a foe, and wring with woe?

Answer:

Hands

Question:

We travel much, yet prisoners are, and close confined to boot. Yet with any horse, we will keep the pace, and will always go on foot.

Answer:

Spurs

Question:

Without a bridle, or a saddle, across a thing I ride a-straddle. And those I ride, by help of me, though almost blind, are made to see.

Answer:

Glasses

Question:

I am the red tongue of the earth, that buries cities.

Answer:

Lava

Question:

I look at you, you look at me, I raise my right, you raise your left.

Answer:

Mirror

Question:

What is the thing which, once poured out, cannot be gathered again?

Answer:

Question:
It is a part of us, and then replaced. It escapes out bodies, to a better place. The world becomes its sizeable home. Its passions unrestraint, the planet it roams.
Answer:
Water

Question:
What word starts with "E", ends with "E", but only has one letter? It is not the letter "E".
Answer:
Envelope

Question:
A hole in a pole, though I fill a hole in white. I'm used more by the day, and less by the night.
Answer:
Eye

Question:
I fly, yet I have no wings. I cry, yet I have no eyes. Darkness follows me. Lower light I never see.
Answer:
Cloud

Question:
I'm full of holes, yet I'm full of water.
Answer:

Question:
Long and slinky like a trout, never sings till it's guts come out.
Answer:
Gun

Question:
What animal keeps the best time?
Answer:
Watchdog

Question:
What kind of room has no windows or doors?
Answer:
Mushroom

Question:
I have legs but walk not, a strong back but work not. Two good arms but reach not. A seat but sit and tarry not.
Answer:
Chair

Question:
It's in your hand though you can not feel it. Only you and time can reveal it.
Answer:
Fate

Question:

133 Not born, but from a Mother's body drawn. I hang until half of me is gone. I sleep in a cave until I grow old. Then valued for my hardened gold.
Answer:
Cheese

Question:
I am the outstretched fingers that seize and hold the wind. Wisdom flows from me in other hands. Upon me are sweet dreams dreamt, my merest touch brings laughter.
Answer:
Feather

Question:
Hands she has but does not hold. Teeth she has but does not bite. Feet she has but they are cold. Eyes she has but without sight.
Answer:
Doll

Question:
Only two backbones and thousands of ribs.
Answer:
Railroad

Question:
Hard iron on horse. Cow's hide on man.
Answer:
Shoe

Question:
What word is the same written forward, backward and upside down?

Answer:
Noon

Question:
I cannot be felt, seen or touched. Yet I can be found in everybody. My existence is always in debate. Yet I have my own style of music.
Answer:
Soul

Question:
I am seen in the water. If seen in the sky, I am in the rainbow, a jay's feather, and lapis lazuli.
Answer:
Blue

Question:
You use it between your head and your toes, the more it works the thinner it grows.
Answer:
Soap

Question:
Fatherless and motherless. Born without sin, roared when it came into the world. And never spoke again.
Answer:
Thunder

Question:
Where can you find roads without cars, forests without trees and cities without houses?

Answer:
Map

Question:
A leathery snake, with a stinging bite. I'll stay coiled up, unless I must fight.
Answer:
Whip

Question:
Take one out and scratch my head, I am now black but once was red.
Answer:
Match

Question:
Mountains will crumble and temples will fall. And no man can survive its endless call.
Answer:
Time

Question:
What has wings, but can not fly. Is enclosed, but can outside also lie. Can open itself up, or close itself away. Is the place of kings and queens and doggerel of every means. What is it upon which I stand? Which can lead us to different lands.
Answer:
Stage

Question:
I'm the source of all emotion, but I'm caged in a white prison.

Answer:
Heart

Question:
I am the tool, for inspiring many. Buy me in the store, for not much more than a penny. Don't overuse me, or my usefulness will go.
Answer:
Pen

Question:
What goes through a door but never goes in. And never comes out?
Answer:
Keyhole

Question:
What goes up when the rain comes down?
Answer:
Umbrella

Question:
I occur twice in eternity. And I'm always within sight.
Answer:
T

Question:
Twigs and spheres and poles and plates. Join and bind to reason make.
Answer:
Skeleton

Question:

The sun bakes them, the hand breaks them, the foot treads on them, and the mouth tastes them.
Answer:
Grapes

Question:
I have many feathers to help me fly. I have a body and head, but I'm not alive. It is your strength which determines how far I go. You can hold me in your hand, but I'm never thrown.
Answer:
Arrow

Question:
What's black when you get it, red when you use it, and white when you're all through with it?
Answer:
Charcoal

Question:
What has four legs in the morning, two legs in the afternoon, and three legs in the evening?
Answer:
Man

Question:
Take off my skin, I won't cry, but you will.
Answer:
Onion

Question:

Hold the tail, while I fish for you.
Answer:
Net

Question:
I am so simple that I can only point. Yet I guide men all over the world.
Answer:
Compass

Question:
Iron roof, glass walls, burns and burns and never falls.
Answer:
Lantern

Question:
Late afternoons I often bathe. I'll soak in water piping hot. My essence goes through. My see through clothes. Used up am I - I've gone to pot.
Answer:
Teabag

Question:
What can't you see, hear or feel, until its too late. What shadows love, and shopkeepers hate?
Answer:
Thief

Question:
What can bring back the dead. Make us cry, make us laugh, make us young. Born in an instant yet lasts a life time?
Answer:

Question:
I have a neck but no head. I have a body but no arm. I have a bottom but no leg.
Answer:
Bottle

Question:
A thousand colored folds stretch toward the sky. Atop a tender strand, rising from the land, until killed by maiden's hand. Perhaps a token of love, perhaps to say goodbye.
Answer:
Flower

Question:
Gold in a leather bag, swinging on a tree, money after honey in its time. Ills of a scurvy crew cured by the sea, reason in its season but no rhyme.
Answer:
Orange

Question:
A slow, solemn square-dance of warriors feinting. One by one they fall, warriors fainting, thirty-two on sixty-four.
Answer:
Chess

Question:
He has married many women but has never married.
Answer:

Question:
In your fire you hear me scream, creaking and whining, yet I am dead before you lay me in your hearth.
Answer:
Log

Question:
I weaken all men for hours each day. I show you strange visions while you are away. I take you by night, by day take you back. None suffer to have me, but do from my lack.
Answer:
Sleep

Question:
I saw a strange creature. Long, hard, and straight, thrusting into a round, dark opening. Preparing to discharge its load of lives. Puffing and squealing noises accompanied it, then a final screech as it slowed and stopped.
Answer:
Train

Question:
I do not breathe, but I run and jump. I do not eat, but I swim and stretch. I do not drink, but I sleep and stand. I do not think, but I grow and play. I do not see, but you see me everyday.
Answer:
Leg

Question:

When liquid splashes me, none seeps through. When I am moved a lot, liquid I spew. When I am hit, color I change. And color, I come in quite a range. What I cover is very complex, and I am very easy to flex.

Answer:

Skin

Question:

Give it food and it will live, give it water and it will die.

Answer:

Fire

Question:

A nut cracker up in a tree.

Answer:

Squirrel

Question:

What happens every second, minute, month, and century. But not every hour, week, year, or decade?

Answer:

N

Question:

It has no top or bottom, but it can hold flesh, bones, and blood all at the same time.

Answer:

Ring

Question:

I am free for the taking. Through all of your life, though given but once at

birth. I am less than nothing in weight, but will fell the strongest of you if held.
Answer:
Breath

Question:
My first is in blood and also in battle. My second is in acorn, oak, and apple. My third and fourth are both the same. In the center of sorrow and twice in refrain. My fifth starts eternity ending here. My last is the first of last, Oh Dear!
Answer:
Barrel

Question:
When I'm metal or wood, I help you get home. When I'm flesh and I'm blood. In the darkness I roam.
Answer:
Bat

Question:
I march before armies, a thousand salute me. My fall can bring victory, but no one would shoot me. The wind is my lover, one-legged am I. Name me and see me at home in the sky.
Answer:
Flag

Question:
Tool of thief, toy of queen. Always used to be unseen. Sign of joy, sign of sorrow. Giving all likeness borrowed.
Answer:
Mask

Question:
What five-letter word becomes shorter when you add two more letters?
Answer:
Short

Question:
What is pronounced like one letter, written with three letters. And belongs to all animals?
Answer:
Eye

Question:
What is it that given one, you'll have either two or none?
Answer:
Choice

Question:
It is greater than God and more evil than the devil. The poor have it, the rich need it, and if you eat it you'll die.
Answer:
Nothing

Question:
What gets bigger the more you take away from it?
Answer:
Hole

Question:
The more of it there is, the less you see.
Answer:

Question:
To cross the water I'm the way, for water I'm above. I touch it not and, truth to say, I neither swim nor move.
Answer:
Bridge

Question:
As beautiful as the setting sun, as delicate as the morning dew. An angel's dusting from the stars. That can turn the Earth into a frosted moon.
Answer:
Snow

Question:
When set loose I fly away. Never so cursed as when I go astray.
Answer:
Fart

Question:
How far will a blind dog walk into a forest?
Answer:
Halfway

Question:
My first is in wield, sever bones and marrow. My second is in blade, forged in cold steel. My third is an arbalest, and also in arrows. My fourth is in power, plunged through a shield. My fifth is in honor, and also in vows. My last will put an end to it all.
Answer:

Question:
Face with a tree, skin like the sea. A great beast I am. Yet vermin frightens me.
Answer:
Elephant

Question:
I am mother and father, but never birth or nurse. I'm rarely still, but I never wander.
Answer:
Tree

Question:
What goes in the water red, and comes out black?
Answer:
Iron

Question:
Grows from the ground, bushes and grass, leaves of yellow, red and brow, unruly plants, get the axe, trim the hedge back down.
Answer:
Hair

Question:
What can touch someone once and last them a life time?
Answer:
Love

Question:
A dragons tooth in a mortals hand, I kill, I maim, I divide the land.
Answer:
Sword

Question:
You will find me with four legs, but no hair. People ride me for hours, but I don't go anywhere without needing to be tugged. Jerked or turned on, I always manage to be ready for work.
Answer:
Desk

Question:
No sooner spoken than broken.
Answer:
Silence

Question:
Though desert men once called me God, today men call me mad. For I wag my tail when I am angry. And growl when I am glad.
Answer:
Cat

Question:
An open ended barrel, it is shaped like a hive. It is filled with the flesh, and the flesh is alive.
Answer:
Thimble

Question:

What kind of pet always stays on the floor?
Answer:
Carpet

Question:
What flies without wings? What passes all things? What mends all sor-row? What brings the morrow?
Answer:
Time

Question:
What has a neck and no head, two arms but no hands?
Answer:
Shirt

Question:
Two in a corner, one in a room, none in a house, but one in a shelter.
Answer:
R

Question:
What does no man want, yet no man want to lose?
Answer:
Work

Question:
I am the heart that does not beat. If cut, I bleed without blood. I can fly, but have no wings. I can float, but have no fins. I can sing, but have no mouth.
Answer:

Wood

Question:
Weight in my belly, trees on my back, nails in my ribs, feet I do lack.
Answer:
Boat

Question:
What is that over the head and under the hat?
Answer:
Hair

Question:
I bind it and it walks. I loose it and it stops.
Answer:
Sandal

Question:
My voice is tender, my waist is slender and I'm often invited to play. Yet wherever I go, I must take my bow or else I have nothing to say.
Answer:
Violin

Question:
Lovely and round, I shine with pale light, grown in the darkness, a lady's delight.
Answer:
Pearl

Question:

The strangest creature you'll ever find has two eyes in front and a hundred behind.
Answer:
Peacock

Question:
A little pool with two layers of wall around it. One white and soft and the other dark and hard. Amidst a light brown grassy lawn with an outline of a green grass.
Answer:
Coconut

Question:
I open wide and tight I shut, Sharp am I and paper-cut fingers too, so do take care, I'm good and bad, so best beware.
Answer:
Scissors

Question:
Only one color, but not one size. Stuck at the bottom, yet easily flies. Present in sun, but not in rain. Doing no harm, and feeling no pain.
Answer:
Shadow

Question:
A house of wood in a hidden place. Built without nails or glue. High above the earthen ground. It holds pale gems of blue.
Answer:
Nest

151

Question:
Who spends the day at the window, goes to the table for meals. And hides at night?
Answer:
Fly

Question:
The beginning of eternity, the end of time and space, the beginning of every end, the end of every place.
Answer:
E

Question:
Always old, sometimes new. Never sad, sometimes blue. Never empty, sometimes full. Never pushes, always pulls.
Answer:
Moon

Question:
I bubble and laugh and spit water in your face. I am no lady, and I don't wear lace.
Answer:
Fountain

Question:
My teeth are sharp, my back is straight, to cut things up it is my fate.
Answer:
Saw

Question:

I love to dance and twist and prance. I shake my tail, as away I sail. Wingless I fly into the sky.
Answer:
Kite

Question:
I usually wear a yellow coat. I usually have a dark head. I make marks wherever I go.
Answer:
Pencil

Question:
My life is often a volume of grief, your help is needed to turn a new leaf. Stiff is my spine and my body is pale. But I'm always ready to tell a tale.
Answer:
Book

Question:
I cost no money to use, or conscious effort to take part of. And as far as you can see, there is nothing to me. But without me, you are dead.
Answer:
Air

Question:
Soldiers line up spaced with pride. Two long rows lined side by side. One sole unit can decide, if the rows will unit or divide.
Answer:
Zipper

Question:

153 What measures out time. Until in time all is smashed to it?
Answer:
Sand

Question:
I turn around once. What is out will not get in. I turn around again. What is in will not get out.
Answer:
Key

Question:
Who is he that runs without a leg. And his house on his back?
Answer:
Snail

Question:
When the day after tomorrow is yesterday. Today will be as far from Wednesday. As today was from Wednesday. When the day before yesterday was tomorrow. What is the day after this day?
Answer:
Thursday

Question:
What has roots as nobody sees, is taller than trees. Up, up it goes, and yet never grows?
Answer:
Mountain

Question:
Come up and let us go. Go down and here we stay.

Answer:
Anchor

Question:
They have not flesh, nor feathers, nor scales, nor bone. Yet they have fingers and thumbs of their own.
Answer:
Gloves

Question:
Long slim and slender. Dark as homemade thunder. Keen eyes and peaked nose. Scares the Devil wherever it goes.
Answer:
Snake

Question:
What is put on a table, cut, but never eaten?
Answer:
Deck

Question:
The sharp slim blade, that cuts the wind.
Answer:
Grass

Question:
Although my cow is dead, I still beat her What a racket she makes!
Answer:
Drum

155

Question:

It sat upon a willow tree, and sang softly unto me. Easing my pain and sorrow with its song. I wished to fly, but tarried long. And in my suffering, the willow was like a cool clear spring. What was it that helped me so? To spend my time in my woe.

Answer:

Bird

Question:

I have four wings but cannot fly. I never laugh and never cry. On the same spot always found, toiling away with little sound.

Answer:

Windmill

Question:

I am never quite what I appear to be. Straight-forward I seem, but it's only skin deep. For mystery most often lies beneath my simple speech. Sharpen your wits, open your eyes, look beyond my exteriors, read me backwards, forwards, upside down. Think and answer the question...What am I?

Answer:

Riddle

Question:

All about the house, with his lady he dances, yet he always works, and never romances.

Answer:

Broom

Question:

I walked and walked and at last I got it. I didn't want it. So I stopped and

looked for it. When I found it, I threw it away.
Answer:
Thorn

Question:
Two in a whole and four in a pair. And six in a trio you see. And eight's a quartet but what you must get. Is the name that fits just one of me?
Answer:
Half

Question:
I drive men mad for love of me. Easily beaten, never free.
Answer:
Gold

Question:
I go around in circles, but always straight ahead. Never complain, no matter where I am led.
Answer:
Wheel

Question:
You use a knife to slice my head. And weep beside me when I am dead.
Answer:
Onion

Question:
Turns us on our backs, and open up our stomachs. You will be the wisest of men though at start a lummox.
Answer:

Question:
Thousands lay up gold within this house. But no man made it. Spears past counting guard this house, but no man wards it.
Answer:
Beehive

Question:
What goes around the world and stays in a corner?
Answer:
Stamp

Question:
What has to be broken before it can be used?
Answer:
Egg

Question:
Creatures of power, creatures of grade, creatures of beauty, creatures of strength. As for their lives, they set everything's pace. For all things must come to live. Under their emerald embrace Either in their life or in their death.
Answer:
Trees

Question:
Double my number, I'm less than a score. Half of my number is less than four. Add one to my double when bakers are near. Days of the week are still greater, I fear.

Answer:
Six

Question:
In buckles or lace, they help set the pace. The farther you go, the thinner they grow.
Answer:
Shoes

Question:
When young, I am sweet in the sun. When middle-aged, I make you gay. When old, I am valued more than ever.
Answer:
Wine

Question:
Forward I'm heavy, but backwards I'm not.
Answer:
Ton

Question:
Hard to catch, easy to hold. Can't be seen, unless it's cold.
Answer:
Breath

Question:
I am two-faced but bear only one. I have no legs but travel widely. Men spill much blood over me. Kings leave their imprint on me. I have greatest power when given away, yet lust for me keeps me locked away.
Answer:

Question:
Two little holes in the side of a hill. Just as you come to the cherry-red mill.
Answer:
Nose

Question:
When you stop and look, you can always see me. If you try to touch, you cannot feel me. I cannot move, but as you near me, I will move away from you.
Answer:
Horizon

Question:
A dagger thrust at my own heart, dictates the way I'm swayed. Left I stand, and right I yield, to the twisting of the blade.
Answer:
Lock

Question:
What instrument can make any sound and be heart, but not touched or seen?
Answer:
Voice

Question:
What goes further the slower it goes?
Answer:
Money

Question:
I can run but not walk. Wherever I go, thought follows close behind.
Answer:
Nose

Question:
Used left or right, I get to travel over cobblestone or gravel. Used up, I vie for sweet success, used down, I cause men great duress.
Answer:
Thumb

Question:
What goes through the door without pinching itself? What sits on the stove without burning itself? What sits on the table and is not ashamed?
Answer:
Sun

Question:
The moon is my father. The sea is my mother. I have a million brothers. I die when I reach land.
Answer:
Wave

Question:
What always goes to bed with his shoes on?
Answer:
Horse

Question:
My thunder comes before the lightning. My lightning comes before the

clouds. My rain dries all the land it touches.
Answer:
Volcano

Question:
My love, when I gaze on thy beautiful face. Careering along, yet always in place, the thought has often come into my mind. If I ever shall see thy glorious behind.
Answer:
Moon

Question:
What starts with a "T", ends with a "T", and has T in it?
Answer:
Teapot

Question:
Today he is there to trip you up. And he will torture you tomorrow. Yet he is also there to ease the pain, when you are lost in grief and sorrow.
Answer:
Alcohol

Question:
I can be moved. I can be rolled. But nothing will I hold. I'm red and I'm blue, and I can be other colors too. Having no head, though similar in shape. I have no eyes - yet move all over the place.
Answer:
Ball

Question:

Inside a burning house, this thing is best to make. And best to make it quickly, before the fire's too much to take!
Answer:
Haste

Question:
What is round as a dishpan, deep as a tub, and still the oceans couldn't fill it up?
Answer:
Sieve

Question:
My first is in some but not in all. My second is into but not in tall. My third in little but no in big. My fourth in port but not in pig. My whole is made in nature's way. For clothing, rugs used every day.
Answer:
Silk

Question:
Gets rid of bad ones, short and tall. Tightens when used, one size fits all.
Answer:
Noose

Question:
What gets wetter the more it dries.
Answer:
Towel

Question:
A little house full of meat, no door to go in and eat.

Answer:
Nut

Question:
A beggar's brother went out to sea and drowned. But the man who drowned had no brother. Who was the beggar to the man who drowned?
Answer:
Sister

Question:
I can be written, I can be spoken, I can be exposed, I can be broken.
Answer:
News

Question:
A horrid monster hides from the day, with many legs and many eyes. With silver chains it catches prey. And eats it all before it dies. Yet in every cottage does it stay. And every castle beneath the sky.
Answer:
Spider

Question:
Five hundred begins it, five hundred ends it. Five in the middle is seen. First of all figures, the first of all letters. Take up their stations between. Join all together, and then you will bring before you the name of an eminent king.
Answer:
David

Question:

Tall in the morning, short at noon, gone at night. But I'll be back soon.
Answer:
Shadow

Question:
What can be heard and caught but never seen?
Answer:
Remark

Question:
I can sizzle like bacon, I am made with an egg. I have plenty of backbone, but lack a good leg. I peel layers like onions, but still remain whole. I can be long, like a flagpole, yet fit in a hole.
Answer:
Snake

Question:
If a man carried my burden, he would break his back. I am not rich, but leave silver in my track.
Answer:
Snail

Question:
High born, my touch is gentle. Purest white is my lace. Silence is my kingdom. Green is the color of my death.
Answer:
Snow

Question:
You heard me before, yet you hear me again, then I die. Until you call me

again.
Answer:
Echo

Question:
What wears a coat in the winter and pants in the summer?
Answer:
Dog

Question:
I'm not really more than holes tied to more holes. I'm strong as good steel,
though not as stiff as a pole.
Answer:
Chain

Question:
I am the third from a sparkle bright, I thrive throughout the day and
night. Deep in the path of a cows white drink. I've had thousands of millions of years to think. But one of my creatures is killing me. And so the
question I ask to thee, is who am I?
Answer:
Earth

Question:
Up on high I wave away but not a word can I say.
Answer:
Flag

Question:
I am whole but incomplete. I have no eyes, yet I see. You can see, and see

right through me. My largest part is one fourth of what I once was.

Answer:

Skeleton

Question:

They're up near the sky, on something very tall. Sometimes they die, only then do they fall.

Answer:

Leaves

Question:

Toss me out of the window. You'll find a grieving wife. Pull me back but through the door, and watch someone give life!

Answer:

N

Question:

A time when they're green. A time when they're brown. But both of these times, cause me to frown. But just in between, for a very short while. They're perfect and yellow. And cause me to smile.

Answer:

Bananas

Question:

I build up castles. I tear down mountains. I make some men blind. I help others to see.

Answer:

Sand

Question:

167 Round as a button, deep as a well. If you want me to talk, you must first pull my tail.
Answer:
Bell

Question:
A house with two occupants, sometimes one, rarely three. Break the walls, eat the boarders, then throw away me.
Answer:
Peanut

Question:
My first master has four legs, my second master has two. My first I serve in life, my second I serve in death. Tough I am, yet soft beside. Against ladies cheeks I often reside.
Answer:
Fur

Question:
I have one eye. See near and far. I hold the moments you treasure and the things that make you weep.
Answer:
Camera

Question:
There are two meanings to me. With one I may need to be broken, with the other I hold on. My favorite characteristic is my charming dimple.
Answer:
Tie

Question:

With sharp edged wit and pointed poise. It can settle disputes without making a noise.

Answer:

Sword

Question:

Lighter than what I am made of, more of me is hidden than is seen. I am the bane of the mariner. A tooth within the sea.

Answer:

Iceberg

Question:

I have one, you have one. If you remove the first letter, a bit remains. If you remove the second, bit still remains. If you remove the third, it still remains.

Answer:

Habit

Question:

Kings and queens may cling to power. And the jester's got his call. But, as you may all discover. The common one outranks them all.

Answer:

Ace

Question:

Glittering points that downward thrust. Sparkling spears that never rust.

Answer:

Icicles

Question:

My first is in fish but no in snail. My second is in rabbit but no in tail. My third is in up but not in down. My fourth is in tiara but not in crown. My fifth is in tree you plainly see. My whole a food for you and me.

Answer:
Fruit

Question:
What I am filled, I can point the way. When I am empty. Nothing moves me. I have two skins. One without and one within.

Answer:
Gloves

Question:
My first is in window but not in pane. My second's in road but not in lane. My third is in oval but not in round. My fourth is in hearing but not in sound. My whole is known as a sign of peace. And from noah's ark won quick release.

Answer:
Dove

Question:
If you drop me I'm sure to crack. But give me a smile and I'll always smile back.

Answer:
Mirror

Question:
I make you weak at the worst of all times. I keep you safe, I keep you fine. I make your hands sweat. And your heart grow cold. I visit the weak, but seldom the bold.

Answer:
Fear

Question:
I run through hills. I veer around mountains. I leap over rivers. And crawl through the forests. Step out your door to find me.
Answer:
Road

Question:
You can see nothing else when you look in my face. I will look you in the eye and I will never lie.
Answer:
Mirror

Question:
I have split the one into five. I am the circle that few will spy. I am the path that breaks and gives. I am the bow no man may bend.
Answer:
Rainbow

Question:
A harvest sown and reaped on the same day in an unplowed field. Which increases without growing, remains whole though it is eaten within and without. Is useless and yet the staple of nations.
Answer:
War

Question:
Snake coiled round and round. Snake deep below the ground. Snake that's

never had a head. Snake that binds but not with dread.
Answer:
Rope

Question:
My first is in ocean but never in sea. My second's in wasp but never in bee. My third is in glider and also in flight. My whole is a creature that comes out at night.
Answer:
Owl

Question:
Dies half its life. Lives the rest. Dances without music. Breathes without breath.
Answer:
Tree

Question:
What runs around all day. Then lies under the bed. With its tongue hanging out?
Answer:
Shoe

Question:
It's true I bring serenity. And hang around the stars. But yet I live in misery, you'll find me behind bars. With thieves and villains I consort. In prison I'll be found. But I would never go to court. Unless there's more than one.
Answer:
S

173

Question:
You must keep this thing. Its loss will affect your brothers. For once yours is lost, it will soon be lost by others.
Answer:
Temper

Question:
What can you catch but not throw?
Answer:
Cold

Question:
Black we are and much admired. Men seek us if they are tired. We tire the horse, comfort man. Guess this riddle if you can.
Answer:
Coal

Question:
I have a face, yet no senses. But I don't really care, because time is of the essence.
Answer:
Clock

Question:
If you have it, you want to share it. If you share it, you don't have it.
Answer:
Secret

Question:
There is one in every corner and two in every room.

Answer:

O

Question:
It comes only before, it comes only after. Rises only in darkness, but rises only in light. It is always the same, but is yet always different.
Answer:
Moon

Question:
As soft as silk, as white as milk, as bitter as gall, a thick green wall, and a green coat covers me all.
Answer:
Walnut

Question:
We are little airy creatures, all of different voice and features, one of us in glass is set. One of us you'll find in jet. Another you may see in tin. And the fourth a box within. If the fifth you should pursue, it can never fly from you.
Answer:
Vowels

Question:
Three little letters. A paradox to some. The worse that it is, the better it becomes.
Answer:
Pun

Question:

176 Almost everyone needs it, asks for it, gives it. But almost nobody takes it.
Answer:
Advice

Question:
Different lights do make me strange, thus into different sizes I will change.
Answer:
Pupil

Question:
Ten men's strength, ten men's length. Ten men can't break it, yet a young boy walks off with it.
Answer:
Rope

Question:
Some try to hide, some try to cheat. But time will show, we always will meet. Try as you might, to guess my name. I promise you'll know, when you I do claim.
Answer:
Death

Question:
I'm a god. I'm a planet. I measure heat.
Answer:
Mercury

Question:
I'm white, I'm round, but not always around. Sometimes you see me,

sometimes you don't.
Answer:
Moon

Question:
People are hired to get rid of me. I'm often hiding under your bed. In time I'll always return you see. Bite me and you're surely dead.
Answer:
Dust

Question:
Die without me, never thank me. Walk right through me, never feel me. Always watching, never speaking. Always lurking, never seen.
Answer:
Air

Question:
White bird, featherless, flying out of paradise. Flying over sea and land. Dying in my hand.
Answer:
Snow

Question:
My life can be measured in hours. I serve by being devoured. Thin, I am quick. Fat, I am slow. Wind is my foe.
Answer:
Candle

Question:
We are all around, yet to us you are half blind. Sunlight makes us invisible,

and difficult to find.
Answer:
Stars

Question:
What's large on Saturday and Sunday. Small on Tuesday, Wednesday, and Thursday, and disappears on Monday and Friday?
Answer:
S

Question:
What do you fill with empty hands?
Answer:
Gloves

Question:
Goes over all the hills and hollows. Bites hard, but never swallows.
Answer:
Frost

Question:
Stealthy as a shadow in the dead of night, cunning but affectionate if given a bite. Never owned but often loved. At my sport considered cruel, but that's because you never know me at all.
Answer:
Cat

Question:
A red drum which sounds without being touched, and grows silent, when it is touched.

Answer:

Heart

Question:

My second is performed by my first, and it is thought a thief by the marks of my whole might be caught.

Answer:

Footstep

Question:

The man who made it didn't need it. The man who bought it didn't use it. The man who used it didn't want it.

Answer:

Coffin

Question:

A hill full, a hole full, yet you cannot catch a bowl full.

Answer:

Mist

Question:

I am a box that holds black and white keys without locks. Yet they can unlock your soul.

Answer:

Piano

Question:

What is often returned, but never borrowed/

Answer:

Thanks

Question:

A muttered rumble was heard from the pen, and I, in my walking stopped to look in. What was this I saw? A massive beast, hoofed, and jawed. With spikes upon its mighty brow, I watched as he struck the turf and prowled. And yet for all of his magnificence, he couldn't get out of that wooden fence.

Answer:

Bull

Question:

What word has kst in the middle, in the beginning, and at the end?

Answer:

Inkstand

Question:

So cold, damp and dark this place. To stay you would refrain, yet those who occupy this place do never complain.

Answer:

Grave

Question:

What kind of nut is empty at the center and has no shell.

Answer:

Doughnut

Question:

I have a title and many pages. I am a genteel of genteel descent. I am a killer veteran of war. I am a slave to my lord pledged to his service.

Answer:

Knight

Question:
Of these things - I have two. One for me - and one for you. And when you ask about the price, I simply smile and nod twice.
Answer:
Sharing

Question:
At night I come without being fetched. By day I am lost without being stolen.
Answer:
Stars

Question:
Ripped from my mother's womb. Beaten and burned, I become a blood thirsty killer.
Answer:
Iron

Question:
I'm very tempting, so its said, I have a shiny coat of red, and my flesh is white beneath. I smell so sweet, taste good to eat, and help to guard your teeth.
Answer:
Apple

Question:
They made me a mouth, but didn't give me breath. Water gives me life, but the sun brings me death.
Answer:
Snowman

181

Question:

I am as simple as a circle. Worthless as a leader, but when I follow a group. Their strength increases tenfold. By myself I am practically nothing. Neither negative or positive.

Answer:

Zero

Question:

I saw a man in white, he looked quite a sight. He was not old, but he stood in the cold. And when he felt the sun, he started to run. Who could he be? Please answer me.

Answer:

Snowman

Question:

We are five little objects of an everyday sort. You will find us all in a tennis court.

Answer:

Vowels

Question:

What always runs but never walks, often murmurs, never talks. Has a bed but never sleeps, has a mouth but never eats?

Answer:

River

Question:

I can be cracked, I can be made. I can be told, I can be played.

Answer:

Joke

183

Question:

My children are near and far. No matter that I know where they are. The gift I give them make their day. But if I were gone they would wander away.

Answer:

Sun

Question:

Screaming, soaring seeking sky. Flowers of fire flying high. Eastern art from ancient time. Name me now and solve this rhyme.

Answer:

Firework

Question:

Who is it that rows quickly with four oars, but never comes out from under his own roof?

Answer:

Turtle

Question:

Who works when he plays and plays when he works?

Answer:

Musician

Question:

My first is twice in apple but not once in tart. My second is in liver but not in heart. My third is in giant and also in ghost. Whole I'm best when I am toast.

Answer:

Pig

Question:

Reaching stiffly for the sky, I bare my fingers when its cold. In warmth I wear an emerald glove and in between I dress in gold.

Answer:

Tree

Question:

A precious stone, as clear as diamond. Seek it out while the sun's near the horizon. Though you can walk on water with its power, try to keep it, and it'll vanish in an hour.

Answer:

Ice

Question:

Half-way up the hill, I see you at last, lying beneath me with your sounds and sights. A city in the twilight, dim and vast, with smoking roofs, soft bells, and gleaming lights.

Answer:

Past

Question:

I heard of a wonder, of words moth-eaten. That is a strange thing, I thought, weird. That a man's song be swallowed by a worm. His blinded sentences, his bedside stand-by rustled in the night - and the robber-guest. Not one wit the wiser. For the words he had mumbled.

Answer:

Bookworm

Question:

Answer:

Question:
Four wings I have, which swiftly mount on high, on sturdy pinions, yet I never fly; And though my body often moves around, upon the self-same spot I'm always found, and, like a mother, who breaks her infant's bread. I chew for man before he can be fed.
Answer:
Windmill

Question:
It flies when it's on and floats coming off.
Answer:
Feather

Question:
What is a foot long and slippery?
Answer:
Slipper

Question:
What has a head, but can't think. And has no limbs but can drive.
Answer:
Hammer

Question:
I'm a lion with a human head. Guess my Riddle or you'll be dead.
Answer:
Sphinx

Question:

A thing with a thundering breech. It weighing a thousand welly. I have heard it roar louder than Guy's wild boar. They say it hath death in its belly.

Answer:

Cannon

Question:

There is a body without a heart. That has a tongue and yet no head. Buried it was before it was made, and loud it speaks and yet is dead.

Answer:

Bell

Question:

Holding two swords and eight spears. Dressed in a cow-leather tunic. He peeks through a hole in the door.

Answer:

Crab

Question:

Little Nancy Etticote, in a white petticoat. With a red nose; the longer she stands, the shorter she grows.

Answer:

Candle

Question:

What needs to be taken from you Before you have it?

Answer:

Picture

187

Question:
Its tall is round and hollow, Seems to get chewed a bit, But you'll rarely see this thing Unless the other end is lit.
Answer:
Pipe

Question:
A red house is made of red bricks. A blue house is made of blue bricks. A yellow house is made of yellow bricks. What is a greenhouse made of?
Answer:
Glass

Question:
Searing 'cross the pitch-black skies, I scream in celebration, Yet moments later, my outburst through, I am naught but imagination.
Answer:
Firework

Question:
I am partially baked. I am not completely lit. I am a portion of the moon. I am lesser than full wit. I am a divider of the hour. I am not a total lie. I am a sibling through one parent.
Answer:
Half

Question:
What has a bottom right at the top?
Answer:
Leg

Question:
What won't break if you throw it off The highest building in the world,
But will break if you place it In the ocean?
Answer:
Tissue

Question:
Though seldom I flatter, I oft show respect To the prelate, the patriot,
and the peer; But sometimes, alas! A sad proof of neglect, Or a mark of
contempt, I appear. By the couch of the sick, I am frequently found, And I
always attend on the dead; With patient affliction, I sit on the ground, But
if talk'd of, I'm instantly fled.
Answer:
Silence

Question:
Though not a plant, has leaves. Though not a beast, has spine. Though
many wouldn't need this thing, It's more valuable than wine.
Answer:
Book

Question:
I'm in a box, full of that which is most rare. But I'm not a flute, and I'm not
some hair. Though soft be my bed, I'm as hard as a rock. While dull in the
dark, I glisten once unlocked.
Answer:
Jewel

Question:
My first is to be seen Every day in the firmament; My second conquers
Kings and queens; And my whole is what I would offer To a friend in dis-

tress.
Answer:
Solace

Question:
If you slash it, It heals at once.
Answer:
Water

Question:
To you, rude would I never be, Though I flag my tongue for all to see.
Answer:
Dog

Question:
The wave, over the wave, a weird thing I saw, Through-wrought, and wonderfully ornate: A wonder on the wave-water became bone.
Answer:
Ice

Question:
What has thirteen hearts But no body or soul?
Answer:
Deck

Question:
A prickly house a little host contains; The pointed weapons keep back from pains, So he, unarmed, safe in his fort remains.
Answer:
Hedgehog

Question:
A small hill with seven holes.
Answer:
Head

Question:
Six legs, two heads, Two hands, one long nose. Yet he uses only four legs Wherever he goes.
Answer:
Horseman

Question:
Plow and hoe, reap and sow, What soon does every farmer grow?
Answer:
Weary

Question:
What jumps when it walks And sits when it stands?
Answer:
Kangaroo

Question:
When we stand up it lies flat. When we lie back it stands up.
Answer:
Foot

Question:
Take one royal word in the plural And make it singular By adding one letter.
Answer:

Question:
I am a tale in children's minds. I keep their secrets and share them inside. I blur their thoughts into fantasies kept Like a canvas of art or a submarine depth. Though an illusion it occurs every night; I give them a fantasy; I give them a fright. Nor good or bad but always nigh?
Answer:
Dream

Question:
I can be short and sometimes hot. When displayed, I rarely impress.
Answer:
Temper

Question:
I have many letters, And though it's strange to say, I stay the same no matter How many I give away.
Answer:
Mailman

Question:
The Load-bearer. The warrior. The Frightened One. The Brave. The Fleet-of-foot. The Iron-shod. The Faithful One. The Slave.
Answer:
Horse

Question:
It has plenty of backbone But doesn't have a let. It peels like an orange But it comes from an egg.

Answer:
Snake

Question:
What does a cat have That no other animal has?
Answer:
Kittens

Question:
I have an eye But cannot see, You'll head inside When you see me.
Answer:
Storm

Question:
It's been around For millions of years, But it's no more Than a month old.
Answer:
Moon

Question:
When I live I cry, If you don't kill me I'll die.
Answer:
Candle

Question:
It's held in the hand When going out.
Answer:
Doorknob

Question:
What kind of dog chases anything red?

Answer:
Bulldog

Question:
Seven brothers, Five work all day, The other two, Just play or pray.
Answer:
Week

Question:
My head bobs lazily in the sun. You think I'm cute For my face is yellow my hair is white and my body is green.
Answer:
Daisy

Question:
My back and belly is wood, And my ribs is lined with leather. I've a hole in my nose and one in my breast, And I'm mostly used in cold weather.
Answer:
Bellows

Question:
I can trap many different things and colors, Ever changing, not boring. Look closely and you may find yourself Also caught in my trap.
Answer:
Mirror

Question:
My first is ocean but not in sea, My second in milk but not in me. My third is in three but not in throw, My fourth in vow but not in crow. My fifth is in eight but not in night, My last is in wrong and also right. My whole is

praise for thoughts or men; Or women, too, or tongue or pen.
Answer:
Clever

Question:
I think you live beneath a roof That is upheld by me; I think you seldom walk abroad, But my fair form you see; I close you in on every side, you very dwelling pave, and probably I'll go with you At last into the grave.
Answer:
Wood

Question:
Six letters do my name compound; Among the aged oft I'm found; The shepherd also, by the brook, Hears me when Leaning on his crook; But in the middle me divide, And take the half on either side, Each backward read, a liquor tell, Ev'ry gay toper knows it well.
Answer:
Murmur

Question:
The side of cat with the most hair.
Answer:
Outside

Question:
Crooked as a rainbow, And slick as a plate, Ten thousand horses Can't pull it straight.
Answer:
River

195

Question:
Two legs I've got, Which never walk on ground; But when I go or run, One leg turns round.
Answer:
Compass

Question:
What's higher than the king?
Answer:
Crown

Question:
The more you look at it, The less you see.
Answer:
Sun

Question:
What is the largest living ant on earth?
Answer:
Elephant

Question:
I have legs but never walk, I may have flowers but no soil, I hold food but never eat.
Answer:
Table

Question:
It increases and decreases Yet no one see it. It is not a fire And yet it can be quenched.

Answer:
Thirst

Question:
Though I do not speak, I oft impart The secret wishes of the heart; I may deceive, may make amends, May create foes, and yet make friends. The harshest anger I can disarm, Such is the power of my charm.
Answer:
Smile

Question:
What was was, before was was was?
Answer:
Is

Question:
A shimmering field that reaches far. Yet it has no tracks, And is crossed without paths.
Answer:
Ocean

Question:
What is the first thing A gardener plants in the garden?
Answer:
Foot

Question:
What bird is always unhappy?
Answer:
Bluebird

Question:
One pace to the North. Two paces to the East. Two paces to the South. Two paces to the West. One pace to the North.
Answer:
Square

Question:
I help to mature your spirits. When moistened I fulfill my purpose. Should I dry out, my task will fail And my quarry may be worthless.
Answer:
Cork

Question:
There is not wind enough to twirl That one red leaf, nearest of its clan, Which dances as often as dance it can.
Answer:
Sun

Question:
Has no feet, but travels far. Is literate, but not a scholar. Has no mouth, yet clearly speaks.
Answer:
Letter

Question:
My first is a heir; My second's a snare; My whole is the offspring of fancy; Which I sent, out of play, Upon Valentine's day, As a token of love, to my Nancy.
Answer:
Sonnet

Question:
What do we see every day, Kings see rarely, And God never sees?
Answer:
Equal

Question:
What is always coming Every day, But never arrives Until the next?
Answer:
Tomorrow

Question:
I'm strangely capricious, I'm sour or I'm sweet, To housewives am useful, To children a treat; Yet I freely confess I more mischief have done, Than anything else That is under the sun.
Answer:
Apple

Question:
We are few to the wise; We are abundant to the drunken; We can calm the beast And are precious to the child; We can devour the heart, Without piercing the skin.
Answer:
Words

Question:
What kind of cheese is made backwards?
Answer:
Edam

Question:

19 Squeeze it and it cries tears As red as its flesh, But its heart is made of stone.
Answer:
Cherry

Question:
Which building has the most stories?
Answer:
Library

Question:
What 's the difference Between one yard and two yards?
Answer:
Fence

Question:
They come to witness the night Without being called, A sailor's guide and a poet's tears. They are lost to the sight each day Without the hand of a thief.
Answer:
Stars

Question:
Black within and red without, With four corners round about.
Answer:
Chimney

Question:
What grows bigger The more you contract it?
Answer:

Question:
It's in the church, but not in the steeple; It's in the parson, but not in the people; It's in the oyster, but not in the shell; It's in the clapper, but not in the bell.
Answer:
R

Question:
Golden treasure I contain, Guarded by hundreds and thousands. Stored in a labyrinth where no man walks, Yet men come often to seize my gold. By smoke I am overcome and robbed, then left to build my treasure anew.
Answer:
Beehive

Question:
When it comes in, From sea to shore, Twenty paces you'll see, No less, no more.
Answer:
Fog

Question:
Has feathers but can't fly. Rests on legs but can't walk.
Answer:
Mattress

Question:
I am merry creature in pleasant time of year, As in but certain seasons, I sing that you can hear; And yet I'm made a by-word, A very perfect mock;

201 Compared to foolish persons, And silliest of all folk.
Answer:
Cuckoo

Question:
Your cat does my first in your ear O were I admitted as near! In my second I've held by you, my fair, So long that I almost despair; But my prey, if at last I overtake, What a glorious third I shall make!
Answer:
Purchase

Question:
A bird done at every meal.
Answer:
Swallow

Question:
What has three feet But no arms or legs?
Answer:
Yard

Question:
Say, what is that which in its form unites All that is graceful, elegant, and true; By all admired, by all acknowledged great, And (as I trust) sincerely loved by you; Which ever on the virtuous attends, And of their peace will surest safeguard prove; The best support of noble, upright minds, The best foundation of connubial love?
Answer:
Truth

203

Question:

What goes with a train, And comes with a train, And the train doesn't need it, But can't go without it?

Answer:

Noise

Question:

You seek it out, When your hunger's ripe. It sits on four legs, And smokes a pipe.

Answer:

Stove

Question:

What fish came first?

Answer:

Goldfish

Question:

I scribble forms of the finest letter, And repel elements of the harshest weather. I am an arrow-aimer and a dust-breaker.

Answer:

Feather

Question:

This is a dead giveaway.

Answer:

Will

Question:

The warmer I am, The fresher I am.

Answer:
Bread

Question:
I know a word of letters three, Add two and fewer there will be.
Answer:
Few

Question:
People want it, And when they have it, They use it, By giving it.
Answer:
Money

Question:
My first keeps time, My second spends time, My whole tells time.
Answer:
Watchman

Question:
I can be quick and then I'm deadly, I am a rock, shell and bone medley. If I was made into a man, I'd make people dream, I gather in my millions By ocean, sea and stream.
Answer:
Sand

Question:
My first, though water, cures no thirst, My next alone has soul, And when he lives upon my first, He then is called my whole.
Answer:
Seaman

205

Question:
I am a good state, There can be no doubt of it; But those who are in, Entirely are out of it.
Answer:
Sane

Question:
What age most travelers have?
Answer:
Baggage

Question:
What is all over the house?
Answer:
Roof

Question:
What can go through glass without breaking it.
Answer:
Light

Question:
Its days are numbered.
Answer:
Calendar

Question:
If you were to throw a white stone into the Red Sea, What would it become?
Answer:

Question:
It doesn't live within a house, nor does it live without. Most will use it when they come in, and again when they go out.
Answer:
Door

Question:
A kind of weather that comes your way, but add a "D" and it will run away.
Answer:
Drain

Question:
I can travel from there to here by disappearing, and here to there by reappearing.
Answer:
T

Question:
There's one of me for everything, through only four are we. O'er and o'er we repeat, cycling endlessly. But Then, I am an act you'll do, when standing at the range. One word, and yet, I've meanings two. I hope it's not too strange.
Answer:
Season

Question:
Though easy to spot, when allowed to plume, It is hard to see, when held

in a room.
Answer:
Smoke

Question:
Cold head and feet; Round as a ball; Always turning around itself.
Answer:
Earth

Question:
An iron horse with a flaxen tail. The faster the horse runs, the shorter his tail becomes.
Answer:
Needle

Question:
In the sun it likes to play; In the rain it goes away; Walk or run it always follows; In the mud it always wallows.
Answer:
Shadow

Question:
I have a little sister, they call her Peep, Peep; She wades the waters deep, deep, deep; She climbs the mountains high,high, high; Poor little creature she has but one eye.
Answer:
Star

Question:
I have no head, and a tail I lack, but oft have arms, and legs, and back; I in-

habit the palace, the tavern, the cot, 'Tis a beggarly residence where I am not. If a monarch were present (I tell you no fable), I still should be placed at the head of the table.

Answer:

Chair

Question:

Be sure to shout for its answers are weak, but there is no language it cannot speak.

Answer:

Echo

Question:

In the evening I'm long, in the morning I'm small; When seen in a ballroom, I'm nothing at all.

Answer:

Shadow

Question:

What becomes too young the longer it exists?

Answer:

Portrait

Question:

What part of a fish weights most?

Answer:

Scales

Question:

What word is that, which, deprived of its first letter, leaves you sick.

Answer:
Music

Question:
I come out of the earth, I am sold in the market. He who buys me cuts my tail, takes off m suit of silk, and weeps beside me when I am dead.
Answer:
Onion

Question:
Though learning has fed me, I know not a letter; I live among the books, Yet am never the better.
Answer:
Bookworm

Question:
I ride, I ride; No tracks are left. I chop and chop; There are no chips left. He rides and rides; Turns around: There is no road left.
Answer:
Boat

Question:
My first is in spell, but not book. My second is in fright and also shook. My third is in cauldron, but never in pot. My fourth is in net and also in knot. My fifth is in bat, but never in vampire. My sixth is in coal, but not found in fire. My seventh is in moon, but not in night.
Answer:
Phantom

Question:

What hatches without food?
Answer:
Hunger

Question:
What is the word that even in plain sight remains hidden?
Answer:
Hidden

Question:
In birth I spring forth, in life I unfold. In death I wilt and die, but rebirth restores all.
Answer:
Leaf

Question:
Slowly creeping, I am weeping, changing shades, and growing.
Answer:
Spring

Question:
Though it is not an ox, it has horns; Though it is not a donkey, it has packed-saddle; And wherever it goes it leaves silver behind.
Answer:
Snail

Question:
What are you certain to find inside your pocket when you reach into it?
Answer:
Hand

211

Question:
I have a tail. I can fly. I'm covered in colorful feathers. I can whistle and I can talk.
Answer:
Parrot

Question:
In Paris but not in France, the thinnest of its siblings.
Answer:
I

Question:
What weeps without eyes or eyelids, her tears rejoicing sons and fathers; and when she laughs and no tears fall, her laughter saddens all hearts?
Answer:
Cloud

Question:
Passed from father to son and shared between brothers, its importance is unquestioned though it is used more by others.
Answer:
Surname

Question:
Within passion's fruit the will be found, and more of them in the pomegranate's crown. Rowed they are within an apple's core, yet other fruits have them more. And though the nectarine has but one, still, this is all just in fun. Playing hide and seek- a children's game. Finding out each player is just the same.
Answer:
Seeds

Question:
What is born long, dies short, and spends its life leaving a trail?
Answer:
Pencil

Question:
A bird that is: Nothing, Twice yourself, Fifty.
Answer:
Owl

Question:
I am nothing really at all, Yet I am easily found; Ignore me at your own peril, and you might end up crowned!
Answer:
Cavity

Question:
I start in little but I end in full, you'll find me in half and complete.
Answer:
L

Question:
What smells the most in the kitchen?
Answer:
Nose

Question:
Old Grandpa Diddle Daddle jumped in the mud puddle, green cap and yellow shoes. Guess all your loftiness and you can't guess these news.
Answer:

Question:
When I get closer my tail grows longer, but when I go away my tail leads the way.
Answer:
Comet

Question:
What is that which, though black itself, enlightens the world without burning?
Answer:
Ink

Question:
What is that which, while it lives, constantly changes its habit, that is buried before it is dead, and whose tomb is valued wherever it is found?
Answer:
Silkworm

Question:
My head and tail both equal are, my middle slender as a bee. Whether I stand on head or heel Is quite the same to you or me. But if my head should be cut off, the matter's true, though passing strange directly I to nothing change.
Answer:
Eight

Question:
My strength is powerful and great, 'Tis tru, altho' it seemeth strange, I car-

ry many thousand weight, with which I many miles do range. Whene'er I reach my journey's end with all my speed I hasten home; and tho' I often man befriend, I sometimes also seal his doom.

Answer:

Tide

Question:

What gets harder to catch the faster you run?

Answer:

Breath

Question:

What turns from red to black as soon as it touches water.

Answer:

Ember

Question:

A path between high natural masses; remove the first letter to get a path between man-made masses.

Answer:

Valley

Question:

Thirty men and ladies two, gathered for a festive do; Dressed quite formal, black and white: soon movement turned to nasty fight.

Answer:

Chess

Question:

What is it that has a power socket on one end and a corkscrew on the

other?
Answer:
Pig

Question:
Shared between two; Most often to woo; Sometimes hot and sometimes cold; The beginning of us all, young and old.
Answer:
Kiss

Question:
What odd number becomes even when beheaded?
Answer:
Seven

Question:
Curtail me thrice, I am a youth; behead me once, a snake; complete, I'm often used, in truth, when certain steps you'd take.
Answer:
Ladder

Question:
What is the thing that stays the same size, but the more it's used the more it decreases?
Answer:
Iron

Question:
Too much for one, Enough for two, and nothing at all for three.
Answer:

Question:
As I was going through a field of wheat, I found something good to eat; It wasn't fish or flesh or bone; I kept it till it ran alone.
Answer:
Egg

Question:
I am small, but, when entire, of force to set a town on fire; Let but one letter disappear, I then can hold a herd of deer; Take one more off, and then you'll find I once contained all human kind.
Answer:
Spark

Question:
It has two bands but no money.
Answer:
River

Question:
It can make rain, but take away one leg and it'll give you pain.
Answer:
R

Question:
Man walks over, man walks under, in times of war he burns asunder.
Answer:
Bridge

217

Question:
What has a coat; Hugs you not in sympathy; Whose smile you'd rather not see; Whose stance is a terrible thing to see; Who is it that brave men run away from; Whose finders are clawed; Whose sleep lasts for months; And who's company we shunt?
Answer:
Bear

Question:
What's at the head of an elephant and at the tail of a squirrel?
Answer:
EL

Question:
Sitting down you have it, Standing up you don't.
Answer:
Lap

Question:
I've got a beautiful, beautiful hall all walled in red velvet, with all white armchairs made of bone, and in the middle a woman dances.
Answer:
Mouth

Question:
My voice rises above the din sometimes catching all unaware. I never ask questions yet get many answers.
Answer:
Doorbell

Question:
What creature starts yellow inside and white outside, then becomes its first five before becoming the whole?
Answer:
Chicken

Question:
I'm a slippery fish in a cloudy sea; Neither hook nor spear will capture me; With your hand you must hunt down this fish, to see that it ends up in the dish.
Answer:
Soap

Question:
When one does not know what it is, then it is something; But when one knows that it is, then it is nothing.
Answer:
Riddle

Question:
What has ears but can't hear?
Answer:
Corn

Question:
This sparkling globe can float on water. It is light as a feather, but ten giants can't pick it up.
Answer:
Bubble

Question:

I fly to any foreign parts, assisted by my spreading wings. My body holds an hundred hearts, Nay, I will tell you stranger things when I am not in haste I ride, and then I mend my pace anon. I issue fire from my side. You witty youths, this riddle con.

Answer:

Ship

Question:

My sides are firmly laced about, Yet nothing is within; you'll think my head is strange indeed, being nothing else but skin.

Answer:

Drum

Question:

As I went over London Bridge I met my sister Jenny; I broke her neck and drank her blood and left her standing empty.

Answer:

Gin

Question:

Perfect with a head, perfect without a head; Perfect with a tail, perfect without a tail; Perfect with either, neither, or both.

Answer:

Wig

Question:

What key is the hardest to turn?

Answer:

Donkey

221

Question:
A young man wants to have it, but when he has it he no longer wants it. Blade in hand he attacks it And does his best to remove it. Yet he knows that it is all in vain.
Answer:
Beard

Question:
By the way, what never moves, wears shoes, sandals and boots, but has no feet?
Answer:
Sidewalk

Question:
It can be repeated but rarely in the same way. It can't be changed but can be rewritten. It can be passed down, but should not be forgotten.
Answer:
History

Question:
What number has all letters in alphabetical order when spelled out?
Answer:
Forty

Question:
My body is quite thin, and has nothing within, neither have I head, face, or eye; yet a tail I have got full as long as- what not? And up, without wings, I can fly.
Answer:
Kite

Question:

In all the world, none can compare, to this tiny weaver, his deadly cloth so silky and fair.

Answer:

Spider

Question:

What bird can lift the heaviest weight?

Answer:

Crane

Question:

They are two brothers. However much they run, They do not reach each other.

Answer:

Wheels

Question:

What is orange and sounds like a parrot?

Answer:

Carrot

Question:

The older they are the less wrinkles they have.

Answer:

Tires

Question:

What is bought by the yard and worn by the foot?

Answer:

Question:
The cost of making only the maker knows, valueless if bought, but sometimes traded. A poor man may give one as easily as king. When one is broken pain and deceit are assured.
Answer:
Promise

Question:
What goes up the chimney down, but can't go down the chimney up?
Answer:
Umbrella

Question:
Four legs in front, two behind; Its steely armor scratched and dented by rocks and sticks; still it toils as it helps feed the hungry.
Answer:
Plough

Question:
Without what would everyone lose their head?
Answer:
Neck

Question:
Bury deep, pile on stones, yet I will dig up the bones.
Answer:
Memory

Question:
Mouth up it gets filled, mouth down it gets empty.
Answer:
Bottle

Question:
What is the end of everything?
Answer:
G

Question:
What goes into the water black and comes out red?
Answer:
Lobster

Question:
Silently I drink and dive in fluids dark as night. I beat the mighty warrior but never in fight. The black blood in my veins your thirst for knowledge slakes. My spittle is more venomous than that of poison snakes.
Answer:
Pen

Question:
A white field, and when it is plowed, its soil is black.
Answer:
Paper

Question:
Held firmly in the hands, like a sword it cuts deep. Bloodless strokes, all, then forward we leap.

Answer:
Paddle

Question:
What has one hand longer than the other, and goes on all day and night.
Answer:
Clock

Question:
It goes up the hill, and down the hill, and yet stands still.
Answer:
Road

Question:
Brown I am and much admired; many horses have I tried; tire a horse and worry a man; tell me this riddle if you can.
Answer:
Saddle

Question:
What do you call the mother-in-law of your sister's husband?
Answer:
Mother

Question:
What is long, pink and wet and is rude to pull out in front of people?
Answer:
Tongue

Question:

A young lady walked through the meadow and scattered her glass pearls. The Moon saw this, yet didn't tell her. The Sun woke up and gathered the pearls.
Answer:
Dew

Question:
Salty water everywhere but not sea in sight!
Answer:
Tears

Question:
I am a window, I am a lamp, I am clouded, I am shining, I am colored and set in white, I fill with water and overflow. I say much, but I have no words.
Answer:
Eye

Question:
What word In the English language is always spelled wrong?
Answer:
Wrong

Question:
Thirty white horses on a red hill, first they champ, then they stamp, then they stand still.
Answer:
Teeth

Question:

227 I reach for the sky, but clutch to the ground. Sometimes I leave, but I am always around.
Answer:
Tree

Question:
Where is the ocean deepest?
Answer:
Bottom

Question:
What goes inside boots and outside shoes?
Answer:
Ankles

Question:
It's always above the negatives Yet it's lower than the first prime no matter how you multiply it's the same every time.
Answer:
Zero

Question:
A precious gift, yet it has no end, no beginning, and nothing in the middle.
Answer:
Ring

Question:
My first is high, my second damp, my whole a tie, a writer's cramp.
Answer:
Hyphen

Question:
My first is a title of honor; My second is myself; My first is your and I; My whole is a beautiful fixed star, seen in the winter.
Answer:
Sirius

Question:
Make three fourths of a cross, then a circle complete; Let two semicircles a perpendicular meet; then add a triangle that stands on two feet, with two semicircles and a circle complete.
Answer:
Tobacco

Question:
What flares up and does a lot of good, and when it dies is just a piece of wood?
Answer:
Match

Question:
My first is an insect; m second is a border; my whole puts the face in a tuneful disorder.
Answer:
Anthem

Question:
At the end of my yard there is a vat, four-and-twenty ladies dancing in that; Some in green gowns, and some with blue hat: He is a wise man who can tell me that.
Answer:
Flax

Question:
A device for finding furniture in the dark.
Answer:
Shin

Question:
While I did live, I food did give, which many one did daily eat. Now being dead, you see they tread me under feet about the street.
Answer:
Cow

Question:
What can you always count on?
Answer:
Fingers

Question:
There she goes over the road, a young mare that is whinnying. A fiery spot on her forehead, with her hindquarters ablaze.
Answer:
Thunder

Question:
The land was white the seed was black It'll take a good scholar to riddle me that.
Answer:
Book

Question:
The strongest chains will not bind it. Ditch and rampart will not slow it

down. A thousand soldiers cannot beat it, it can knock down trees with a single bush.
Answer:
Wind

Question:
They took me from my mother's side where I was bravely bred and when to age I did become they did cut off my head. They gave to me some diet drink that often made me mad but it made peace between two kings and made two lovers glad.
Answer:
Quill

Question:
In the fields a frightful thing. Watch it and you will find, it has a pitchfork in the front, and a broom back behind.
Answer:
Bull

Question:
Walk on the living, they don't even mumble. Walk on the dead, they mutter and grumble.
Answer:
Leaves

Question:
When people come for me to meet, they come to me with heavy feet. The one I hold, when I get my chance, will turn and spin, and start to dance.
Answer:
Gallows

Question:
I have legs but seldom walk; I backbite many but never talk; I seek places that can hide me because those that feed me cannot abide me.
Answer:
Flea

Question:
First I may be your servant's name; then your desires I may proclaim; And, when your mortal life is over hold all your wealth within my power.
Answer:
Will

Question:
A hold leading in a hold leading out I connect to a cavern that is slimy throughout.
Answer:
Nose

Question:
What can you spell with B, R and Y?
Answer:
Brandy

Question:
You can draw me, fire me or fill me in.
Answer:
Gun

Question:
A father's child, a mother's child, yet no one's son.

Answer:
Daughter

Question:
Although a human shape I wear, Mother I never had; And though no sense nor life I share, in finest silks I'm clad. By every miss I'm valued much, beloved and highly prized; still my cruel fate is such by boys I am often despised.
Answer:
Doll

Question:
What flowers have two lips?
Answer:
Tulips

Question:
It can pierce the best armor and make swords crumble with a rub, yet for all its power It can't harm a wooden club.
Answer:
Rust

Question:
Though my beauty is becoming I can hurt you just the same; I come in many colors; I am what I am by any other name.
Answer:
Rose

Question:
The older this thing grows the more valued it becomes. It is always much

better when its breathing is done.
Answer:
Wine

Question:
Before my birth I have a name, but soon as born I lose the same; and when I'm laid within the tomb, I do my father's name assume; I change my name three days together, yet live but on in any weather.
Answer:
Today

Question:
What is drawn by everyone without pen or pencil?
Answer:
Breath

Question:
I am the beginning of sorrow, and the end of sickness. You cannot express happiness without me, yet I am in the midst of crosses. I am always in risk, yet never in danger. You may find me in the sun, but I am never seen out of darkness.
Answer:
S

Question:
My first is nothing but a name; my second is more small; my whole is of so little fame it has no name at all.
Answer:
Nameless

235

Question:
Slain to be saved, with much ado and pain, scatter'd, dispersed and gather'd up again; wither'd though young, sweet though not perfumed, and carefully laid up to be consumed.
Answer:
Hay

Question:
In many hall ways you would stand, if not with this in hand.
Answer:
Key

Question:
When the horse strokes the cat the wood begins to sing.
Answer:
Violin

Question:
The answer to this riddle is unknown.
Answer:
Unknown

Question:
What stays the same size no matter how much they weight?
Answer:
Scales

Question:
They belong to me; they belong to you; they can make you feel happy or make you feel blue; they never end until the day you do.

Answer:
Thoughts

Question:
What is brown and sticky?
Answer:
Stick

Question:
The higher I climb the hotter I engage, I cannot escape my crystal cage.
Answer:
Mercury

Question:
I'm sometimes white, but most often I'm black. I take you there, but never bring you back.
Answer:
Hearse

Question:
There was a little heart inside a little white house, which was inside a little yellow house, which was inside a little brown house, which was inside a little green house.
Answer:
Walnut

Question:
Sometimes black, sometimes white, I have veins but no blood.
Answer:
Marble

Question:
I have a head and a tail, exactly the same size.
Answer:
Coin

Question:
If you're to idleness inclined, a lesson take from me; though small in body, yet you'll find I work with constant glee. And lest stern Winter's chilling snow should spread the verdure over; While Summer's sun in full glow, I then secure my store.
Answer:
Ant

Question:
What can you blow up and keep intact?
Answer:
Balloon

Question:
As I walked along the path I saw something with four fingers an done thumb, but it was not flesh, fish, bone, or fowl.
Answer:
Glove

Question:
When I'm born I fly. When I'm alive I lay. When I'm dead I run.
Answer:
Snow

Question:

What divides by uniting and by dividing?
Answer:
Scissors

Question:
They can be long or short; they can be grown or bought; they can be painted or left bare; they can be round or square.
Answer:
Nails

Question:
Long Legs, crooked thighs, little head, and no eyes.
Answer:
Tongs

Question:
I am where the sky is orange, I am where the glass is red, I am the land of violet bananas and the home to blue oranges.
Answer:
Negative

Question:
Gown but not a priest; crown but not a king.
Answer:
Rooster

Question:
My tail is long, my coat is brown, I like the country, I like the town. I can live in a house or live in a shed, And I come out to play when you are in bed.
Answer:

Mouse

Question:
What follows a dog wherever it goes?
Answer:
Tail

Question:
It is by nature, soft as silk; A puffy cloud, white as milk; Snow tops this tropical crop; The dirtiest part of a mop.
Answer:
Cotton

Question:
The floor's on top, the roof's beneath, and from this place I rarely leave. Yet with the passing of each day. A new horizon greets my gaze.
Answer:
Sailor

Question:
We dwell in cottages of straw, and labor much for little gains; sweet food from us our masters draw, and then with death reward our pains.
Answer:
Bees

Question:
What English word retains the same pronunciation, even after you take away four of its five letters?
Answer:
Queue

Question:
Even if my life is taken eight still remain.
Answer:
Cat

Question:
What kind of cup doesn't hold water?
Answer:
Cupcake

Question:
Four holes, one going in and three coming out; When you are going in you are out and when you are coming out you are in.
Answer:
Shirt

Question:
What is never eaten before lunch?
Answer:
Dinner

Question:
My first is snapping, snarling, growling, My second's industrious, romping, and prowling. Higgledy piggledy Here we lie, picked and plucked, and put in a pie.
Answer:
Currants

Question:
What kind of fish chases a mouse?

Answer:
Catfish

Question:
We are little brethren twain, arbiters of loss and gain; man to our counters run, some are made, and some undone; but men find it, to their cost, few are made, but numbers lost; though we play them tricks for ever, yet they always hope our favor.
Answer:
Dice

Question:
Where do penguins come from?
Answer:
Eggs

Question:
It goes up, but at the same time goes down Up toward the sky, and down to the ground. It's present tense and past tense too, Come for a ride, just me and you.
Answer:
Seesaw

Question:
What liquid can contain the soul?
Answer:
Ink

Question:
Looks like water, but it's heat. Sits on sand, lays on concrete. A play on the

eyes, but it's all lies.
Answer:
Mirage

Question:
In wealth I abound; in water I stand; as a fencer I'm valued all over the land; at Venice I'm famous; by farmers I'm prized; respected by law, yet huntsmen despised; consternation and ruin ensue when I break; And the beasts of the forest advantage won't take.
Answer:
Bank

Question:
What sphinxes employ and players enjoy.
Answer:
Riddle

Question:
His eyes were raging, that scraggly beast. His lips were bursting, with rows of angry teeth. Upon his back a razor was found. It was a fearsome battle we fought, my life – or his, one would be bought. And when we were through, and death chilled the air, we cut out his heart, and ate it with flair.
Answer:
Boar

Question:
This is a coat that will soon dry but it must be put on while it is wet.
Answer:
Paint

Question:
Besides Paris, what is the capital of France?
Answer:
F

Question:
Though blind as well, can lead the blind well.
Answer:
Cane

Question:
If two is company and three is a crowd, what are four and five?
Answer:
Nine

Question:
I view the world in little space, am always changing place; No food I eat, but, by my power, procure what millions do devour.
Answer:
Sun

Question:
Can not be bought, can not be sold, even if it's made of gold.
Answer:
Heart

Question:
Despite having long teeth, every bit of food it grabs gets taken from it.
Answer:
Fork

Question:

My first, if you do, you'll increase; my second will keep you from heaven; my whole, such a human caprice, is more frequently given than taken.

Answer:

Advice

Question:

Oh lord! I am not worthy! I bend my limbs to the ground. I cry, yet without a sound. Let me drink of waters deep. And in silence I will weep.

Answer:

Willow

Question:

A hundred years I once did live, and often wholesome food did give, yet all that time I ne'er did roam, so much as a half a mile from my home, my days were spent devoid of strife, until at last I lost my life. And since my death – I pray give ear, I oft have traveled far and near.

Answer:

Tree

Question:

My first is a term to relate a circumstance present or past; and those who are much prone to prate, my second will spout away fast. My whole, in the days of our youth, is what we extremely despised; and though it say nothing but truth, yet it never need hope to be prized.

Answer:

Telltale

Question:

They try to beat me, they try in vain. And when I win, I end the pain.

Answer:

Question:
What animal has feet on the head?
Answer:
Lice

Question:
What occurs four times in every week, twice in every month, only once in a year but never in a day?
Answer:
e

Question:
Runs smoother than any rhyme, loves to fall but cannot climb.
Answer:
Rain

Question:
It's the only vegetable or fruit that is never sold frozen, canned, processed, cooked, or in any other form but fresh.
Answer:
Lettuce

Question:
I saw a fight the other day; A damsel did begin the fray. She with her daily friend did meet, then standing in the open street, she gave such hard and sturdy blows, he bled ten gallons at the nose; yet neither seemed to faint nor fall, nor gave her an abuse at all.
Answer:

Question:
What do rich people have that can be changed into the law.
Answer:
Wealth

Question:
It's red, blue, purple, and green, no one can reach it, not even the queen.
Answer:
Rainbow

Question:
Man of old, it is told would search until he tired, not for gold, ne'er be sold, but what sought he was fire. Man today, thou mayst say, has quite another aim, in places deep, he did seek, to find me for his gain!
Answer:
Oil

Question:
A vessel have I, that is round as pear, moist in the middle, surrounded with hair; and often it happens that water flows there.
Answer:
Eye

Question:
Poke your fingers in my eyes and I will open wide my jaws. Linen cloth, quills, or paper, my greedy lust devours them all.
Answer:
Scissors

Question:
The more holes you cover the lower it goes.
Answer:
Recorder

Question:
What is the middle of water but is not an island.
Answer:
T

Question:
Has its teeth on your head but doesn't bite.
Answer:
Comb

Question:
Where can you add two to eleven and get one as the correct answer?
Answer:
Clock

Question:
What is common to eat before it's born and after it's dead?
Answer:
Chicken

Question:
Sometimes it glitters, but often not; May be cold, or may be hot! Ever changing though the eye can't measure, concealed within are many treasures. Some find safety beneath its gate, while some may die beneath its weight! Old and broken, it brings forth life.

Answer:
Rock

Question:
What hole do you mend with holes?
Answer:
Net

Question:
Before a circle appear, twice twenty-five, and five in rear; One fifth of eight subjoin; and then you'll quickly find what conquers men.
Answer:
Love

Question:
I tremble at each breath of air, and yet can heaviest burdens bear.
Answer:
Water

Question:
It has no legs to dance, it has no lungs to breathe, it has no life to live or die, and yet it does all three.
Answer:
Fire

Question:
What loses its head in the morning and gets it back at night?
Answer:
Pillow

Question:
What word has three syllables and twenty six letters?
Answer:
alphabet

Question:
A single syllable do I claim, black was my most famous name; Fetal to mortals here below, thousands have I slain in a single blow.
Answer:
Plague

Question:
My first a blessing sent to earth, of plants and flowers to aid the birth; my second surely was designed to hurl destruction on mankind; my whole a pledge from pardoning heaven, of wrath appeased and crimes forgiven.
Answer:
Rainbow

Question:
I am born in fear, raised in truth, and I come to my own in deed. When comes a time that I'm called forth, I come to serve the cause of need.
Answer:
Courage

Question:
Green but not a lizard, white without being snow, and bearded without being a man.
Answer:
Leek

251

Question:
It is in every mountain, it's not in any hill, it's not in all the world, and yet it's in the mill.
Answer:
M

Question:
Barren location, infertile and dry; my name means "to leave", it's not heard to see why.
Answer:
Desert

Question:
What is between heaven and earth?
Answer:
And

Question:
Those wooden birds are now in sight whose voices roar, whose wings are white, whose maws are fill'd with hose and shoes, with wine, cloth, sugar, salt and news, when they have eas'd their stomachs here they cry farewell, until next year.
Answer:
Ships

Question:
A word there is of plural number, foe to ease and tranquil slumber; with any other word you take, to add an "s" would plural make. But if you add an "s" to this, how strange the metamorphosis: What plural was, is plural now no more, and sweet, what bitter was before.
Answer:

Question:

I war with the wind, with the waves I wrestle; I must battle with both when the bottom I seek, my strange habitation by surges o'er-roofed. I am strong in strife, while I still remain; as soon as I stir, they are stronger than I. They wrench and they wrest, till I run from my foes; what was put in my keeping they carry away.

Answer:

Anchor

Question:

What fish is a celebrity?

Answer:

Starfish

Question:

My first is in riddle, but not in little. My second is in think, but not in brink. My third is in thyme, but not in time. My fourth is in mother, but not in brother. My last is in time, but no t in climb.

Answer:

Rhyme

Question:

Though it be cold, I wear no clothes, the frost and snow I never fear; I value neither shoes nor hose, And yet I wander far and near: My diet is forever good, I drink no cider, port, nor sack, what Providence doth send for food, I neither buy, nor sell, nor lack.

Answer:

Fish

253

Question:
This thing can bat but never hit. It is next to a ball that is never thrown. It is good luck when found and it falls when it is lost.
Answer:
Eyelash

Question:
In almost every house I'm seen, (No wonder then I'm common) I'm neither man, nor maid, nor child, nor yet a married woman. I'm penniless and poor as Job, Yet such my pride by nature, I always wear a kingly robe, though a dependent creature.
Answer:
Cat

Question:
My first is a slice affords so nice; my second discomposes; my whole's a bed where honor's head devotedly reposes.
Answer:
Hammock

Question:
My love for Eliza shall never know my first; neither shall it be my second; but it shall be my whole.
Answer:
Endless

Question:
I'm not a bird, but I can fly through the sky. I'm not a river, but I'm full of water.
Answer:
Cloud

Question:
What king can you make if you take the head of a lamb, the middle of a pig, the hind of a buffalo, and the tail of a dragon?
Answer:
Lion

Question:
My first is equality; my second is inferiority; my whole is superiority.
Answer:
Peerless

Question:
You can read it both ways, I wear; One way it's a number, reversed a snare.
Answer:
Ten

Question:
It stands on one leg with its heart in its head.
Answer:
cabbage

Question:
There is a word in the English language, the two first letters signify a male, the three first a female, the four first a great man, and the whole a great woman.
Answer:
heroine

Question:
Put into a pit, locked beneath a grate, guarded through the night, yet it

still goes out.
Answer:
Fire

Question:
What fruit is of great use in history?
Answer:
Date

Question:
My first is second in line; I send shivers up your spine; not quite shining bright I glitter in the light.
Answer:
Ice

Question:
As I went across the bridge, I met a man with a load of wood which was neither straight nor crooked. What kind of wood was it?
Answer:
Sawdust

Question:
What goes up and down without moving?
Answer:
Stairs

Question:
There's not a kingdom on the earth, but I have traveled over and over, and though I know not whence my birth, yet when I come, you know my roar. I through the town do take my flight, and through the fields and mead-

ows green, and whether it be day or night, I neither am nor can be seen.
Answer:
Wind

Question:
My first brace Nelson yielded, midst the jar of angry battle, and the din of war; my second, when from labor we retreat, far form polite, yet offers us a seat; my whole is but my second more complete.
Answer:
Armchair

Question:
Has a tongue, but never talks. Has no legs, but sometimes walks.
Answer:
Shoe

Question:
what leaps one time out of four?
Answer:
Year

Question:
How do snails travel?
Answer:
Slowly

Question:
Though I have neither legs nor feet, my use is for to go; Altho' I cannot speak, I tell what others want to know.
Answer:

Watch

Question:
What has green hair, a round red head and a long thin white beard?
Answer:
Radish

Question:
What can you add to a bucket full of water to make it lighter?
Answer:
Hole

Question:
The more you take the more you leave behind.
Answer:
Steps

Question:
My parents are singers, and while my father has red hair I am pale and completely bald.
Answer:
Egg

Question:
There is someone, and there is always another, for without the other, there wouldn't be one.
Answer:
Twins

Question:

A man who worked in a butcher shop was six feet tall and wore size eleven shoes. What did he weigh?
Answer:
Meat

Question:
A useful thing, hard, firm, and white, outside in shaggy robe bedight; Hallowed within right cleverly, it goes to work both white and dry. When after labor it comes back, you'll find it moist and very black; for service it is ready ever, and fails the hand that guides it never.
Answer:
Pen

Question:
In Spring I look gay, Decked in comely array, In Summer more clothing I wear; when colder it grows, I filing off my clothes, and in winter quite naked appear.
Answer:
Tree

Question:
Locked up inside you and yet they can steal it from you.
Answer:
Heart

Question:
Men seize it form its home, tear apart its flesh, drink the sweet blood, then cast its skin aside.
Answer:
Orange

259

Question:
Bold are the first; true are the second; playful are the third; clever are the fourth; forceful are the fifth.
Answer:
BRAVE

Question:

Answer:

Question:
I can be caught but not thrown
Answer:
Cold

Question:
I can travel the world without leaving my corner. What am I?
Answer:
Stamp

Question:
What can be measured but not seen?
Answer:
Time

Question:
What is always coming but never really arrives?
Answer:
Tomorrow

261

Question:
If you have me, you want to share me. But if you share me, you'll lose me.
What am I?
Answer:
Secret

Question:
I am a three letter word. Add two more letters and you'll have fewer.
What word am I?
Answer:
Few

Question:
What has a tongue but no mouth?
Answer:
Shoe

Question:
I can run but not walk, have a mouth but can't talk, and a bed but I do not
sleep. What am I?
Answer:
River

Question:
I weigh nothing, but you can see me, and if you put me in a bucket, I'll
make it lighter
Answer:
Hole

Question:

I can be told, I can be played. I can be cracked, and I can be made. What am
I?
Answer:
Joke

Question:
What kind of coat is best put on wet?
Answer:
Paint

Question:
What animal jumps when it walks, and sits when it stands?
Answer:
Kangaroo

Question:
What surrounds everyplace, is the beginning of the end, and the end of
time and space?
Answer:
E

Question:
I can be found in seconds, minutes and centuries, but not in days, years or
decades
Answer:
N

Question:
The more of this you have the less you see. What is it?
Answer:

Question:
What has a head and tail but no limbs or body?
Answer:
Coin

Question:
What grows when fed but dies when watered?
Answer:
Fire

Question:
What is lighter than what it is made of?
Answer:
Ice

Question:
What has many keys but unlocks no doors?
Answer:
Piano

Question:
What looks back but cannot see?
Answer:
Reflection

Question:
What is it that can have the whole taken from it and still be left with some?

Answer:
Wholesome

Question:
What kind of nail can be grown?
Answer:
Fingernail

Question:
What has a neck but no head and two arms but no hands?
Answer:
Shirt

Question:
The more of these you take, the more you leave behind. What are they?
Answer:
Footsteps

Question:
What is never thirsty but always drinking and alive but never breathing?
Answer:
Fish

Question:
What is lighter than air but can never be lifted?
Answer:
Bubble

Question:
If you drop me, I'll crack, but if you smile, I'll smile back. What am I?

Answer:
Mirror

Question:
I do not speak, but there is no word I cannot make. What am I?
Answer:
Alphabet

Question:
What has an end but no beginning, a home but no family, and a space without room?
Answer:
Keyboard

Question:
What never asks questions but receives a lot of answers?
Answer:
Telephone

Question:
What stays on the ground but never gets dirty?
Answer:
Shadow

Question:
What surrounds the world yet exists in a thimble
Answer:
Space

Question:

What happens four times in every week, twice every month and once in a year?
Answer:
E

Question:
I'm tall in the morning and short in the noon. I disappear at night but I will be back soon
Answer:
Shadow

Question:
What breaks in the water but never on land?
Answer:
Wave

Question:
What kind of room has no doors or windows?
Answer:
Mushroom

Question:
What can be broken without being touched?
Answer:
Promise

Question:
What starts with and ends with 'e' but only has one letter in it?
Answer:
Envelope

Question:
If you take off my skin, I will not cry, but you will. What am I?
Answer:
Onion

Question:
What goes up and down without moving?
Answer:
Temperature

Question:
What can be filled with empty hands?
Answer:
Gloves

Question:
What gets served but never eaten?
Answer:
Tennis Ball

Question:
I cannot be used until I have been broken. What am I?
Answer:
Egg

Question:
What word is pronounced the same even after removing 4 of its 5 letters?
Answer:
Queue

Question:

What cries without a voice, flutters without wings, and bites without a mouth?

Answer:

Wind

Question:

What do the poor have that the rich need, and if you eat it, you will die?

Answer:

Nothing

Question:

What is pronounced as one letter, written with three, and is the same forwards and backwards?

Answer:

Eye

Question:

What can be seen but not touched?

Answer:

Shadow

Question:

How can the letters OWONDER be rearranged to make one word?

Answer:

One word

Question:

What falls but never breaks?

Answer:

Question:
What breaks without falling?
Answer:
Day

Question:
What has fingers and a thumb but no hand?
Answer:
Glove

Question:
What can be any size or shape and gets bigger the more you take from it?
Answer:
Hole

Question:
I have a face but no eyes and hands but no arms. What am I?
Answer:
Clock

Question:
What does everyone have that goes up but never comes down?
Answer:
Age

Question:
What makes my left hand my right?
Answer:

Question:
I am made of the stuff around me but lighter than it. I am more hidden than seen. What am I?
Answer:
Iceberg

Question:
Where can you add 2 to 11 and get 1?
Answer:
Clock

Question:
My maker doesn't want me, my buyer doesn't use me and my user will never see me
Answer:
Coffin

Question:
What is better than the best thing and worse than the worst thing?
Answer:
Nothing

Question:
What should you keep after giving?
Answer:
Your Word

Question:

What has a ring but no fingers?
Answer:
Telephone

Question:
I have been around for millions of year, but I am never more than a month old
Answer:
Moon

Question:
What can go up the chimney down but can't go down the chimney up?
Answer:
Umbrella

Question:
I am put on a table, cut, but never eaten
Answer:
Cards

Question:
What is full of holes but still holds water?
Answer:
Sponge

Question:
This man has married many but has never been married
Answer:
Priest

RIDDLE BOOK FOR KIDS

Question:
Not my sister nor my bother but still the child of my mother
Answer:
Myself

Question:
Many hear me, but no one sees me, and I only speak when spoken to
Answer:
Echo

Question:
I never was but am always to be, and everyone looks forward to me
Answer:
Future

Question:
What goes up and down the stairs without moving?
Answer:
Rug

Question:
There are millions of me. I am very small but when moving fast I am deadly?
Answer:
Sand

Question:
What comes down but never back goes up?
Answer:
Rain

Question:
Tall when I'm young but short when I'm old
Answer:
Candle

Question:
What goes up when the rain comes down?
Answer:
Umbrella

Question:
What word becomes shorter when you add two letters to it
Answer:
Short

Question:
I have two hands but cannot clap
Answer:
Clock

Question:
If you walk into a cabin with a match, a kerosene lamp and a fireplace, which do you light first?
Answer:
Match

Question:
how many months have 28 day?
Answer:
Twelve

Question:
I have an eye but cannot see. What I am?
Answer:
Needle

Question:
what can go through tows and over hills without moving?
Answer:
Road

Question:
what loses its head every morning only to get it back every night?
Answer:
Pillow

Question:
I am a word with six letters. Subtract 1 of these letters and you have 12.
what am I?
Answer:
Dozens

Question:
what goes up and down without moving?
Answer:
Stairs

Question:
A farmer has 17 sheep and all but 9 run away. how many are left?
Answer:
Nine

Question:
I can shave everyday but my beard will stay. who am I?
Answer:
Barber

Question:
what grows in winter, dies in summer and grows roots upward?
Answer:
Icicle

Question:
how far can you walk into the woods?
Answer:
Halfway

Question:
I am your mother's brother's only brother in law. who am I?
Answer:
Father

Question:
what word contains all 26 letter?
Answer:
Alphabet

Question:
taken from a mine and shut in a wooden case, and yet used by almost everybody. what am I?
Answer:
Lead

Question:
how many $5 bills are in a dozen?
Answer:
Twelve

Question:
what has a neck but no head?
Answer:
Bottle

Question:
what eight letter word has kst in middle, in the beginning and at the end?
Answer:
Inkstand

Question:
before Mt. Everest was discovered, what was the tallest mountain in the world?
Answer:
Mt. Everest

Question:
What always comes into the house through the keyhole?
Answer:
Key

Question:
I am everywhere but cannot be seen captured or held, only heard, what am I?
Answer:

Question:
what is bought by the yard and worn by the foot?
Answer:
Carpet

Question:
I have a metal roof and glass wall. I burn and burn but never fall. what am I?
Answer:
Lantern

Question:
I am liquid in nature but don't me to far, for then I may break and my damage may scar
Answer:
Glass

Question:
what has four legs and a back but no body?
Answer:
Chair

Question:
what must take a bow before it can speak?
Answer:
Violin

Question:

what has one foot on each side and one in the middle?

Answer:

Yardstick

Question:

what word can be written forward, backward or upside down

Answer:

Noon

Question:

nightly they come without being fetched? What are they?

Answer:

Stars

Question:

what falls when thrown up but rises when thrown down?

Answer:

Ball

Question:

you can swallow me, but I can also swallow you

Answer:

Water

Question:

how many bricks does it take to finish a brick building?

Answer:

One

Question:

you use this from your head to your toes. the more you use it the thinner it
grows
Answer:
Soap

Question:
what has a tongue but cannot talk, gets around a lot but cannot walk?
Answer:
Shoe

Question:
what goes with a car, comes with a car, is no use to a car, but the car can't
move without it?
Answer:
Noise

Question:
how many seconds are there in a year?
Answer:
Twelve

Question:
what binds two people yet touches only one?
Answer:
Ring

Question:
I am larger than castle, lighter than air, yet a thousand men could not
move me
Answer:

Question:
it stand on one leg and have my heart in my head
Answer:
Cabbage

Question:
I am round as a bowl, deep as a tub, but all the world's water couldn't fill
me up
Answer:
Sieve

Question:
What is found once in a second, once in a minute, twice in a millennium,
but never in a year?
Answer:
N

Question:
They are dark and always on the run. But without the sun, there would be
none. they are
Answer:
Shadows

Question:
What does someone else have to take before you can get?
Answer:
Photograph

281

Question:
When filled I can point the way. But when empty unmoving I stay. What am I?
Answer:
Glove

Question:
What runs but cannot walk?
Answer:
Nose

Question:
What has teeth but no mouth?
Answer:
Saw

Question:
I carry my home on my back. I am not rich, but I leave silver in my track. What am I?
Answer:
Snail

Question:
what has four legs but no feet and two arms but no hand?
Answer:
Chair

Question:
What disappears if you say its name?
Answer:

Question:
I cab be full, but I will never spill. I disappear at times, but return I always will. What am I?
Answer:
Moon

Question:
What has no beginning or end and nothing in the middle?
Answer:
Doughnut

Question:
What has one foot but no body?
Answer:
Ruler

Question:
If you have me, you want to share me. But if you share me, you lose me. What am I?
Answer:
Secret

Question:
What is the only animal without the ability to fly but still does?
Answer:
Man

Question:

283What flies when it born, lies while it is alive, and runs when it dies?
Answer:
Snowflake

Question:
I cannot be felt or moved, but as you come closer, I get more distant. What am I
Answer:
Horizon

Question:
What did Adam and Eve lack that everyone else has?
Answer:
Parents

Question:
I am bigger than elephant but lighter than a feather. What am I?
Answer:
Wind

Question:
For most, I am fast. For others, I am slow. An obsession to all, I make the world go. What am I?
Answer:
Time

Question:
When they are caught they are thrown away when they escape you itch
What am I?
Answer:

Question:
There is an old invention still used today that allows one to look through walls. What is it?
Answer:
Window

Question:
What is red, blue, purple and green that no one can reach, not even the queen?
Answer:
Rainbow

Question:
What is brown and has a head and a tail but no legs?
Answer:
Penny

Question:
What is yours, but your friends use it more than you do?
Answer:
Your Name

Question:
If you have three oranges and take away two, how many will you have?
Answer:
Two

Question:

285   I am weightless, yet no man can hold me for long. What am I?
Answer:
Breath

Question:
What is round, has a twin, and sees more than most?
Answer:
Eye

Question:
This is a shape and a symbol that we literally cannot live without. What is it?
Answer:
Heart

Question:
I dance and sing in the breeze, but I have neither voice nor feet. What am I?
Answer:
Tree

Question:
Neither bought nor sold but more valuable than gold. It is built but not by hand. What is it?
Answer:
Trust

Question:
In the ground I am nothing, but give me time and I'll be something. What am I?

Answer:
Seed

Question:
What can provide food before it is alive, while it is alive and after it's dead?
Answer:
Chicken

Question:
What hangs in the sky by day but at night goes away?
Answer:
Sun

Question:
Without me where would you be? I am not your eyes, but I help you see. What am I?
Answer:
Light

Question:
What points the way without a hand. It floats on water but exists on land?
Answer:
Compass

Question:
What has four wings but cannot fly and uses the wind but does not know why?
Answer:
Windmill

287

Question:
A locked sphere without hinges or key. Break me open and golden treasures you'll see
Answer:
Egg

Question:
My life only lasts hours as I quickly become devoured. Fast or slow, wind is my foe. What am I?
Answer:
Candle

Question:
If you held me for too long, you would die. What am I?
Answer:
Breath

Question:
The day before two days after the day before tomorrow is Saturday. What day is it today?
Answer:
Friday

Question:
Glittering points that downward thrust. Sparkling spears that do not rust. What is it?
Answer:
Icicle

Question:

What makes a loud noise when changing its jacket and get larger in the process but weighs less after?
Answer:
Popcorn

Question:
What is green, has four legs, no tail, and usually heard at night?
Answer:
Frog

Question:
Man greatly desires me. I am easily beaten but never free. What am I?
Answer:
Gold

Question:
What is seen in the water and in the sky? It is part of the rainbow and can be in your eye.
Answer:
Blue

Question:
You will hear me again. I will not appear until you call me.
Answer:
Echo

Question:
What is gentle enough to soothe the skin and light enough to exist in the sky but strong enough to break rocks?
Answer:

Water

Question:
I will not be what I am until the man who made me dies. What am I?
Answer:
Prince

Question:
What do people need but always give away?
Answer:
Money

Question:
You don't want this, but if you have it, you don't want to lose it. What is it?
Answer:
Lawsuit

Question:
Men walk over me but boats go under me. What am I?
Answer:
Bridge

Question:
I am too much for one but not enough for two. Give me to a third and I am gone. What am I?
Answer:
Secret

Question:
What holds names and memories which are not its own?

Answer:
Gravestone

Question:
What can be hot or cold and appears blue but is really red?
Answer:
Blood

Question:
Bill's mom has four kids: Mary, John, and Alice. What is the name of her fourth child?
Answer:
Bill

Question:
It is able to speak because it has a hard gone. You know what it is as soon as it has sung. What is it?
Answer:
Bell

Question:
What is flat, usually square, and made from trees but isn't wood?
Answer:
Paper

Question:
I am very large but look very small. When night falls, I am cherished by all. What am I?
Answer:
Star

291

Question:
I am hot then cold, a liquid then solid, and I am at once flaky and wet.
What am I?
Answer:
Wax

Question:
Never swallowed but certainly chewed, tossed in the mouth but it is not
food. What is it?
Answer:
Gum

Question:
What building has the most stories?
Answer:
Library

Question:
What becomes whiter the dirtier it gets?
Answer:
Chalkboard

Question:
What turns everything around but does not move?
Answer:
Mirror

Question:
What is something you can hold without ever touching?
Answer:

Question:
I am sometimes white but usually black. I take you there, but I never bring you back. What am I?
Answer:
Hearse

Question:
I have roads but no pavement, rivers but no water, and cities but no buildings. What am I?
Answer:
Map

Question:
What is filled with air and sometimes a gas, tied to a string and often seen on your birthday?
Answer:
Balloon

Question:
What vegetable is never sold canned, frozen, or cooked, only fresh?
Answer:
Lettuce

Question:
What can be played with no rules and no winners or losers?
Answer:
Instruments

293

Question:
What is eaten but not grown and was born in water but will disappear if soaked?
Answer:
Salt

Question:
I come in many shapes and colors. I sing in the breeze but only live 7 months. What am I?
Answer:
Leaf

Question:
Born from a fountain of wealth, I am black instead of gold but valued the same. What am I?
Answer:
Oil

Question:
A container holding water but not a cup. If you want to find me, look up. What am I?
Answer:
Coconut

Question:
What comes from an egg and peels like a fruit? It can sizzle like bacon and slender to boot.
Answer:
Snake

Question:

What is always wet but never rusts and often held but mostly untouched?

Answer:

Tongue

Question:

My life is a volume of joy and grief, but I need your help to turn a new leaf.
What am I?

Answer:

Book

Question:

What weakens a man for hours each day and presents you strange visions
while you're away?

Answer:

Sleep

Question:

I am set in white but colored myself. I have no words, but I reveal much.
What am I?

Answer:

Eye

Question:

I am wingless but airborne, and when I meet your gaze tears will fall from
your eyes. What am I?

Answer:

Smoke

Question:

295 My treasures are golden and guarded by thousands amongst a maze no man can enter. What am I?
Answer:
Beehive

Question:
What travels from house to house and is sometimes narrow and sometimes wide but always stays outside?
Answer:
Path

Question:
What has a brown coat, a long tail, and lives in house or shed but most active while you're in bed?
Answer:
Mouse

Question:
A place with substance and story, where many masquerade to there glory. What am I?
Answer:
Stage

Question:
What has no arms, hands, or legs but moves the earth?
Answer:
Worm

Question:
I have a red cap on my head and a stone in my throat my sweetness is

something of note. What am I?
Answer:
Cherry

Question:
You may have many of me but never enough. After the last one arrives you will have no more. What am I?
Answer:
Birthday

Question:
What devours all and can kill a king. Destroy a town and crushes mountains down?
Answer:
Time

Question:
If I turn my head, you may go where you want, but if I turn again, you could stay and rot. What am I?
Answer:
Key

Question:
As your ideas grow, I shrink. What am I?
Answer:
Pencil

Question:
I am partly blind but can still see. I have legs but use them only for sleeping? What am I?

Answer:
Bat

Question:
What is something yet nothing, but if you fill it up it will disappear?
Answer:
Hole

Question:
Even though I am far from the point and make no mistakes of my own, I fix yours. What am I?
Answer:
Eraser

Question:
I am not alive but seem so, because I dance and breathe with no legs or lungs of my own. What am I?
Answer:
Flame

Question:
I am blinding at times yet help you see. I am necessary, but you'll burn with too much of me. What am I?
Answer:
Sunlight

Question:
I am at your hand when it is dark and hidden away in the light. What am I?
Answer:

Question:
I have arms but cannot carry a thing. But wave at me and I wave back at you. What am I?
Answer:
Reflection

Question:
What covers its face with its hands, speaks no language, yet most known what it's saying?
Answer:
Clock

Question:
Its thunder comes before lightning, it's lightning before clouds, and its rain dries all it touches. What is it?
Answer:
Volcano

Question:
I am found by the ocean and offer you a bed. Whether you want me or not, to your house I am led?
Answer:
Sand

Question:
Born in a shell I adorn your neck. What am I?
Answer:
Pearl

299

Question:
A man without bones whose flesh is cold. A man unthinking who is always shrinking. Who is he?
Answer:
Snowmen

Question:
What has armor but is not a knight, snaps but is not a twig, and is always at home even on the move?
Answer:
Turtle

Question:
I have two legs, but they only touch the ground while I'm at rest. What am I?
Answer:
Wheelbarrow

Question:
I enclose you in darkness but allow you to see many things. If you resist me, you're likely to get rings. What am I?
Answer:
Sleep

Question:
I can feel any space, float, and disappear. Never touching the ground I help others get around. What am I?
Answer:
Gas

Question:

I am black as night but can be filled with light. Through me things can be seen, although it is a screen. What am I?

Answer:

Television

Question:

Green on the outside but red and black inside. I am food but mostly liquid. What am I?

Answer:

Watermelon

Question:

I am part of the bird that is not in the sky. I can swim in the water but always stay dry. What am I?

Answer:

Shadow

Question:

What build its house with earthen string and ensnares its prey with a biting sting?

Answer:

Spider

Question:

I am a container with an inside golden that can't be opened unless I am broken. What am I?

Answer:

Egg

301

Question:
What runs distances and make many turns along the way, yet it never moves one foot?
Answer:
Watch

Question:
I can fill a house or fill your mouth but you can never catch me in your hands. What am I?
Answer:
Smoke

Question:
What is part of you and all around you but if it entangles you, it will kill you?
Answer:
Water

Question:
I remain unseen but hold many things, and when you are making a decision you consult me. What am I?
Answer:
Mind

Question:
I am sometimes yellow and sometimes white. Half of me is dark and the other is light. What am I?
Answer:
Moon

Question:
I am always with my partner, and I make noise that you never see me create. What am I?
Answer:
Thunder

Question:
I have a long tail that I let fly. Every time I go through a gap, I leave a bit of my tail in the trap. What am I?
Answer:
Needle

Question:
You take my clothes off when you put your clothes on. What am I?
Answer:
Hanger

Question:
I am bushy headed but have no air. No moisture will not enter my skin, but it's good at keeping it in. What am I?
Answer:
Tree

Question:
Place your fingers in my eyes, and I will open my jaws to devour paper and cloth. What am I?
Answer:
Scissors

Question:

303 In the morning I sing on feathered wing. I soar through the air without a care. What am I?
Answer:
Bird

Question:
What has four legs but cannot move without help?
Answer:
Chair

Question:
Add me to myself and multiply by 4. Divide me by 8 and you will have me once more. What number am I?
Answer:
Any number

Question:
Four years ago. Alex was twice as old as Jake. Four years from now. Jake will be 3/4 of Alex's age. How old is Alex?
Answer:
Twelve

Question:
We are two brothers on opposite sides of the road, but we never see each other. Who are we?
Answer:
Eyes

Question:
What can your pocket hold while it is completely empty?

Answer:
Hole

Question:
What can be a tree but also part of your hand?
Answer:
Palm

Question:
We total ten, but two we make. When we are together people may quake.
What are we?
Answer:
Fists

Question:
What is used by man, tossed by trees, everywhere but unseen?
Answer:
Air

Question:
This can only be given and never bought, it is craved by sinners but by
saints it is not? What is it?
Answer:
Forgiveness

Question:
I have two bodies, but I am joined into one. I sit still, but when flipped I
run. What am I?
Answer:
Hourglass

305

Question:
Man walks over, and man swims under. It times of war, it can be burned asunder? What is it?
Answer:
Bridge

Question:
This is a paradox to some. The worse it is the better it becomes. What is it?
Answer:
Pun

Question:
I may be dropped in dry, but I come out wet. The longer I stay, the stronger I get. What am I?
Answer:
Teabag

Question:
Where force can't get through, I with a gentle movement do. What am I?
Answer:
Key

Question:
I have no end and am the ending of all that begins. What am I?
Answer:
Death

Question:
What speeds on a track but isn't in a race and has a whistle to announce its steady pace?

Answer:
Train

Question:
This has no beginning, middle or end, and all the greatest thinkers see it but can't comprehend. What is it?
Answer:
Space

Question:
What comes once a day but leaves every morning?
Answer:
Night

Question:
Of these everyone has ten, part of two wholes at the arms end. What are they?
Answer:
Fingers

Question:
In the forest, this blends in just right, but every December it is covered with lights. What is it?
Answer:
Evergreen

Question:
2 people in front of 2 people. 2 people behind 2 people, and 2 people beside 2 people. How many people are there?
Answer:

Question:
I am the number nine you see. Before 100, how many will you count of me?
Answer:
Twenty

Question:
I am long and thin and make things right. I will repair your mistake but watch my bite. What am I?
Answer:
Needle

Question:
I can fill a room but take up no space. Look out at night, and I am in no place. What am I?
Answer:
Light

Question:
I give life for my own, have a beginning, but my end is unknown. What am I?
Answer:
Sun

Question:
What can speak without a tongue and listen without ears?
Answer:
Telephone

309

Question:
Round like a cup but deep like a well. To make it sing, you must pull its tail.
What is it?
Answer:
Bell

Question:
They can float and tickle, but their sound is rarely heard unless you're a pillow or bird. What are they?
Answer:
Feathers

Question:
I live in the corn, and my job is to deter. Free from pests your crops I assure. What am I?
Answer:
Scarecrow

Question:
A hand without flesh and nothing can I hold. My grip cannot be used until I am sold. What am I?
Answer:
Gloves

Question:
Pointing North, South, East, and West it saves the lost and helps the rest. What is it?
Answer:
Compass

Question:

Usually green but can be brown. It's a great place to play or lie down.
What is it?

Answer:

Grass

Question:

A circle of stones, never in rows. Stacked one on the other, mystery it sows. What is it?

Answer:

Stonehenge

Question:

Through its wounds, water does run. It once held many but now has none.
What is it?

Answer:

Shipwreck

Question:

A beacon from home to guide your way. It can be a lifesaver on a stormy day. What is it?

Answer:

Lighthouse

Question:

What travels from coast to coast without ever moving?

Answer:

Highway

Question:

311 You can't live without doing this, and we all do it at the same time. Yet many wish it wasn't happening. What is it?
Answer:
Aging

Question:
What kind of table has no legs?
Answer:
Periodic

Question:
What has numbers on the outside but letters inside?
Answer:
Mailbox

Question:
In a tree you'll find me moving slow as can be. My name is a sin but from them I am free. What am I?
Answer:
Sloth

Question:
A father's and mother's child I am one, but I am no one's son. Who am I?
Answer:
Daughter

Question:
I bring milk and have a horn, but I am not a cow. What am I?
Answer:
Milk Truck

Question:

In two years I know, I'll be twice as old as five years ago, said Tom. How old is Tom?

Answer:

Twelve

Question:

A book once owned by the wealthy, now rare to find. Never for sale and often left behind. What am I?

Answer:

Phonebook

Question:

At first I am a yellow weed in the lawn, and then the wind blows, and my white feathers are gone. What am I?

Answer:

Dandelion

Question:

With four oars it swims but it is always at home. Its back is like armor, tougher than chrome. What is it?

Answer:

Turtle

Question:

I can burn your mouth and sting your eye, but I am consumed everyday. What am I?

Answer:

Salt

313

Question:
With hands that can't hold and eyes that can't see, she's cherished by some but has no real family. Who is she?
Answer:
Doll

Question:
I can bring back the dead and a tear to your eye. A stir of emotions will follow close by. What am I?
Answer:
Memories

Question:
My body is timber and I am a boy among men. I have a nose without end and an insect for a friend. Who am I?
Answer:
Pinocchio

Question:
What do you use to hoe a row and say hello?
Answer:
Hands

Question:
Agile on my feet, I drive dogs mad. I flick my tail when I'm angry and hum when I'm glad. What am I?
Answer:
Cat

Question:

You need a key to receive an answer from me. The answer you'll find is straight from your mind. What is it?
Answer:
Code

Question:
I am in your hand but you don't hold me. After some time, you will know me. What am I?
Answer:
Fate

Question:
Grown in darkness yet shimmers in light. It is lovely, round, and every woman's delight. What is it?
Answer:
Pearl

Question:
I am young in the sun and trapped to be aged. Held in a bottle but opening is delayed. What am I?
Answer:
Wine

Question:
My uses are changing, but I still remain the same. My interior is quiet, and stories are my game. What am I?
Answer:
Library

Question:

315 I spin and hum, I'm your summer tool. Just flip the switch, and I serve to cool. What am I?
Answer:
Fan

Question:
More rare today than long ago. There's a salutation from friends written below. What am I?
Answer:
Letter

Question:
What can get you there in eco style, pushed by your legs mile after mile?
Answer:
Bicycle

Question:
Secured in place, I work undercover, and with a flick of your finger. My purpose you'll discover. What am I?
Answer:
Light bulb

Question:
What is eaten by man, served among many, grown by many, and white as snow?
Answer:
Rice

Question:
I live next to beauty trying to catch your eye. Grab me without looking,

and you're surely to cry. What am I?
Answer:
Thorn

Question:
Without feather or wing I fly, but you'll known what I am when I hover near by. What am I?
Answer:
Helicopter

Question:
What starts out in a field and then crashed on a stone. It becomes much more when to the fire it's thrown?
Answer:
Bread

Question:
What is born on the ground but floats to the sky, to be returned back again from the clouds up high?
Answer:
Rain

Question:
It gets passed among men and builds without growing. It serves to injure from a source unknowing. What is it?
Answer:
Lie

Question:
What has a green top, red on its belly, seeds on the outside, and tastes

great in jelly?
Answer:
Strawberry

Question:
Sometimes it's silver but also gold. Printed on paper it's a treasure to hold.
What is it?
Answer:
Currency

Question:
Strip the skin under my skin, and my flesh you'll reveal. It tastes sweet and tart, now throw out the peel. What is it?
Answer:
Orange

Question:
He calls in the morning, the day to renew, if his owner gets hungry, he'll be turned to stew. What is he?
Answer:
Rooster

Question:
I am a number with a couple of friends, quarter a dozen, and you'll find me again. What am I?
Answer:
Three

Question:
Tucked out of sight. I sing best at night. No instrument around, but you'll

find me on the ground. What am I?
Answer:
Cricket

Question:
Grown in the ground, it's taller than you. Strip off the outside, the yellow pieces you chew. What is it?
Answer:
Corn

Question:
What moves across the land but never has to steer? It has delivered our goods year after year. What is it?
Answer:
Train

Question:
Built of metal or wood to divide. It will make us good neighbors, if you stay on your side. What is it?
Answer:
Fence

Question:
Tickle with your fingers and a song it will sing. Be careful, though, you may break a string. What is it?
Answer:
Guitar

Question:
It is a place of play on a sunny day. Winter will come and take all the fun,

but we'll be back in May. What is it?
Answer:
Park

Question:
It can be grown in your yard or bought at the store and is given for love when less is more?
Answer:
Flower

Question:
If you give it a tug, you can sit in the dark. Tug it again and a light will spark. What is it?
Answer:
Lamp

Question:
Controlled by your hands and feet. It would be nothing without a street. What is it?
Answer:
Car

Question:
It carries paper of the most important sort but also plastic, I'm glad to report. What is it?
Answer:
Wallet

Question:
You use this to clean although it is small. If you forget it, your smile will

appall? What is it?
Answer:
Toothbrush

Question:
What comes in many varieties and can't be seen or touched, but it often makes you move?
Answer:
Music

Question:
Touch this and you'll regret it. But if it's cold, you won't forget it. What is it?
Answer:
Fire

Question:
What relies on columns but isn't a house, and asks for help but can't speak itself?
Answer:
Newspaper

Question:
What is not a ball but yet a sphere, and holds all lands and people year after year?
Answer:
Earth

Question:
Give it a toss, and it's ready, but not until it's dressed. What is it?

Answer:
Salad

Question:
What can stand in place of a country but still fold away in a drawer?
Answer:
Flag

Question:
What is made of wood and metal and must be buried before it works?
Answer:
Shovel

Question:
Not a comb or a brush but makes the hair feel plush. What is it?
Answer:
Shampoo

Question:
What has a bell but isn't a church. Is full of air but is not a balloon?
Answer:
Trumpet

Question:
It comes from crystal and melts to a treat. Add it to your tea to make it sweet. What is it?
Answer:
Sugar

Question:

What can be grown without sun or soil and can either provide nourishment or deliver poison?

Answer:

Mushroom

Question:

Never alive but practically extinct. How we miss the letters pressing the ribbon of ink. What is it?

Answer:

Typewriter

Question:

What zips through the sky with a tail of fire and dust. It could be an omen, its origin to discuss?

Answer:

Comet

Question:

It stands upright and can be quite grand. Its secret is not hidden but right at hand. What is it?

Answer:

Piano

Question:

What is light enough to float but will stay in a pack and may save your life if its on your back?

Answer:

Parachute

Question:

323 My mother is water and my brother the sky. I am grey when wet but white when dry. What am I?
Answer:
Cloud

Question:
What lives where it can breathe and has a hole in its back?
Answer:
whale

Question:
Stolen from a cow, I'm placed in a vat. My flavor gets stronger the longer I've sat. What am I?
Answer:
Cheese

Question:
I contain words about words, some of which you've never heard. What am I?
Answer:
Dictionary

Question:
What has a spine, tail, and leash but isn't a dog?
Answer:
Kite

Question:
Small was my stature, but my success was great. Until I entered Belgium to be handed my fate. Who am I?

Answer:
Napoleon

Question:
A flash of light on a grey day. If you're made of metal, you best stay away. What am I?
Answer:
Lightning

Question:
Used on a diamond and left on a board. It's great for a gymnast his grip to restore. What is it?
Answer:
Chalk

Question:
What walks on 4 legs when young, 2 when grown, and 3 when old?
Answer:
Man

Question:
You toss the outside and cook the inside. Then, you eat the outside and toss the inside. What is it?
Answer:
Corn

Question:
You can break me, and I still work. If you touch me, you're mine. What am I?
Answer:

Question:
At the sound of me, you may stomp your feet, but you may also dream or weep. What am I?
Answer:
Music

Question:
What starts with T, ends with T, and has T in it?
Answer:
Teapot

Question:
You saw me where I could not be. Yet, often you see me. What am I?
Answer:
Reflection

Question:
I can be round or shot, painted or bare. Sometimes I am round, at others I'm square. What am I?
Answer:
Fingernail

Question:
Before I came, the world was darker, that's true. But beware, I can also kill you. What am I?
Answer:
Electricity

327

Question:
It keeps you on the ground and stops things from floating around. What is it?
Answer:
Gravity

Question:
What is found in the woods, and if you're not careful can become part of your skin?
Answer:
Sliver

Question:
This only turns over once you have travelled very far. What is it?
Answer:
Odometer

Question:
A mile from end to end, but easily found on the face of a friend. What is it?
Answer:
Smile

Question:
It can't be seen or felt. It can't be touched or smelt. Behind stars and under hills. All emptiness it fills. What is it?
Answer:
Space

Question:
What has weight in its belly and trees on its back, nails in it's ribs and a

liquid track?
Answer:
Boat

Question:
Two is one, four is two, and six is three. Don't you see? What am I?
Answer:
Half

Question:
At night I'm a mountain but in the morning a meadow. What am I?
Answer:
Bed

Question:
I can help you to mend. I hide my body but never my head. What am I?
Answer:
Nail

Question:
I am always around, but in the morning I show. You'll know its me from my golden glow. What am I?
Answer:
Sunlight

Question:
What instrument can make any sound but not be seen or touched?
Answer:
Voice

329

Question:
I met a man and drew his name. He tipped his hat and played my game.
What is his name?
Answer:
Andrew

Question:
I am in the middle of water but not an island. What am I?
Answer:
T

Question:
A snake that binds without a head. A snake of fiber no need to dread.
What am I?
Answer:
Rope

Question:
What has skin of stone and tongue of wood, a belt of water and long as stood?
Answer:
Castle

Question:
I am not eaten or baked, but I'm sure you'll find that some problems are solved with me in mind. What am I?
Answer:
Pi

Question:

Attracted by light but flies at night. It's wind and hairy but not too scary.
What is it?
Answer:
Moth

Question:
Found in pizza but also the sky. You'll know I'm around when I'm close by.
What am I?
Answer:
Circle

Question:
I sometimes lack reason but often rhyme. I'm not the best but a good way
to pass time. What am I?
Answer:
Riddle

Question:
I am very important, but often overlooked. What am I?
Answer:
Nose

Question:
Always wooden and covered in paint. It can make you laugh or hide, be-
cause something dark is inside. What is it?
Answer:
Pencil

Question:
I can invent dreams or open the skies. It's easy to use me, just close your

eyes. What am I?
Answer:
Imagination

Question:
Covered in stone and sun. It's home to many but also none. What is it?
Answer:
Cemetery

Question:
I'm on the end of a hook or combined with book. What am I?
Answer:
Worm

Question:
Only one foot tall but I govern you. What am I?
Answer:
Ruler

Question:
I can be found on a present, the front of a boat, or after the rain. What am I?
Answer:
Bow

Question:
I cover reality and hide what is true but may bring out the courage in you. What am I?
Answer:
Make up

Question:

For me, much blood has been shed. I have two faces but only bare one head. What am I?

Answer:

Coin

Question:

I rise up free the first and second time. But need me a third, and I will cost you. What am I?

Answer:

Teeth

Question:

I cannot walk and cannot see, I'm straw on a stick but keep things tidy. What am I?

Answer:

Broom

Question:

I can be used to type and point you see. But don't forget, you can count on me. What am I?

Answer:

Fingers

Question:

What dresses for summer and sheds in the winter?

Answer:

Tree

Question:

332. What is as large as a mountain or small as a pea and endlessly swims in a waterless sea?
Answer:
Asteroid

Question:
What can hold all days, weeks, and months but still fit on a table?
Answer:
Calendar

Question:
What must be looked through in order to see?
Answer:
Glasses

Question:
What has two spines and a lot of ribs, and carries much but never moves?
Answer:
Train Tracks

Question:
I bind it, it walks. I loosen it stops. What is it?
Answer:
Sandal

Question:
The cloud is my mother, my father the wind. The lake is my son and the rainbow my bed. What am I?
Answer:
Rain

Question:

What is heavy forward but not backward?

Answer:

Ton

Question:

The more I dry the wetter I get. What am I?

Answer:

Towel

Question:

What can travel around the world while staying in a corner?

Answer:

Stamp

Question:

If you have me, you want to share me. If you share me, you haven't got me. What am I?

Answer:

Secret

Question:

Take off my skin – I won't cry, but you will! What am I?

Answer:

Onion

Question:

If I drink, I die. If I eat, I am fine. What am I?

Answer:

Fire

335

Question:
I run distances, often making many turns, yet I never move one foot.
What am I?
Answer:
Watch

Question:
You answer me, although I never ask you questions. What am I?
Answer:
Phone

Question:
The more it dries, the wetter it gets. What is it?
Answer:
Towel

Question:
What goes up and down without moving?
Answer:
Stairs

Question:
At night they come without being fetched. By day they are lost without being stolen. What are they?
Answer:
Stars

Question:
The thunder comes before the lightning; the lightning comes before the clouds. The rain dries everything it touches.

Answer:
Volcano

Question:
Never was, am always to be. No one ever saw me, nor ever will. And yet I am the confidence of all, to live and breath on this terrestrial ball. What am I?
Answer:
Future

Question:
It regulates our daily movements, but it feels no interest in our lives. It directs us when to come and go, but does not care if we pay attention. What is it?
Answer:
Clock

Question:
If you drop a yellow hat in the Red Sea what does it become?
Answer:
Wet

Question:
What has to be broken before it can be used?
Answer:
Egg

Question:
What do you fill with empty hands?
Answer:

Gloves

Question:
Who spends the day at the window, goes to the table for meals and hides at night?
Answer:
Fly

Question:
I bind it and it walks. I loose it and it stops
Answer:
Sandal

Question:
It stands on one leg with its heart in its head.
Answer:
Cabbage

Question:
It's been around for millions of years, but it's no more than a month old.
What is it?
Answer:
Moon

Question:
What is it that you will break even when you name it?
Answer:
Silence

Question:

Owned by Old McDonald.

Answer:

Farm

Question:

If a dog were filling out a resume, he might list his mastery of this game under skills

Answer:

Fetch

Question:

Sleep-inducing melody.

Answer:

Lullaby

Question:

This guy crossed a road and everyone wants an explanation.

Answer:

Chicken

Question:

A storage facility for criminals and fire-breathing reptiles.

Answer:

Dungeon

Question:

Cute hares that hop and deliver eggs at Easter are called b this nickname.

Answer:

Bunny

339

Question:
What is it the more you take away the larger it becomes?
Answer:
Hole

Question:
Poorly behaved children often find themselves sitting in these.
Answer:
Corners

Question:
Teenage girls are pros at causing this.
Answer:
Drama

Question:
It has a face and two hands but no arms or legs.
Answer:
Clock

Question:
Who are the two brothers who live on opposite sides of the road yet never see each other?
Answer:
Eyes

Question:
What holds water yet is full of holes?
Answer:
Sponge

Question:
Lives without a body, hears without ears, speaks without a mouth, to which the air alone gives birth.
Answer:
Echo

Question:
When one does not know what it is, then it is something; but when one knows what it is, then it is nothing.
Answer:
Riddle

Question:
What goes into the water black and comes out red?
Answer:
Lobster

Question:
A beautiful succession of sounds.
Answer:
Music

Question:
You are having a bad day if 12 peers deem you to be this.
Answer:
Guilty

Question:
A small paradise surrounded by dry heat. Some have Wonderwalls.
Answer:

Question:
Mad bats and dogs carry this.
Answer:
Rabies

Question:
Nature's way of applauding a lightning strike.
Answer:
Thunder

Question:
Lives in winter, dies in summer and grows with its root upwards.
Answer:
Icicle

Question:
Pan's nemesis.
Answer:
Hook

Question:
A tasty reward given to well behaved dogs and kids.
Answer:
Treat

Question:
These animals hang out in the mist.
Answer:

Question:
The signature stroll of ducks and penguins.
Answer:
Waddle

Question:
Brings you May flowers.
Answer:
Showers

Question:
Consuming food would be pretty tough without these chompers.
Answer:
Teeth

Question:
Surname of the pilot of the Millennium Falcon.
Answer:
Solo

Question:
Where jewelery pierces your head.
Answer:
Lobe

Question:
If you blow past your destination, you'll have to throw your car into this.
Answer:

Reverse

Question:
You can do this with your friends. You can do this with your nose. But don't do it with your friend's nose!
Answer:
Pick

Question:
Each of these ends in a kettle full of precious metal and the double variety is quite awesome.
Answer:
Rainbow

Question:
These help engines spin and trousers stay up.
Answer:
Belt

Question:
A twiggy home.
Answer:
Nest

Question:
Very helpful if you intend to go gently down a river.
Answer:
Rowboat

Question:

A shower that lights up the sky.
Answer:
Meteor

Question:
This is needed both for courage and hard-cover books.
Answer:
Spine

Question:
A defendant will go free if a reasonable amount of this exists.
Answer:
Doubt

Question:
Godzilla calls this place home.
Answer:
Japan

Question:
This would be a good place to find Can-Can girls and drunk Cowboys.
Answer:
Saloon

Question:
Known for tuxedo and marching.
Answer:
Penguin

Question:

345   Dark, feathery, and popular in Baltimore and fantasy books.
Answer:
Ravens

Question:
They bring oxygen into blood.
Answer:
Lungs

Question:
Boxes marked as this should not be abused.
Answer:
Fragile

Question:
This creature travels in a gaggle.
Answer:
Goose

Question:
Flavors your food and divides the year up.
Answer:
Season

Question:
Can be heard in court or used to carry briefs.
Answer:
Case

Question:

Has a strong attraction to belly buttons.
Answer:
Lint

Question:
These nutrients are vital to your health.
Answer:
Vitamin

Question:
Greedy grumpy holiday hater.
Answer:
Scrooge

Question:
Everyone claims to know a way to stop these involuntary contractions.
None of them works.
Answer:
Hiccup

Question:
According to the ads, this is the favorite beverage of friendly polar bears.
Answer:
Coke

Question:
Flavors range from strawberry to toe.
Answer:
Jam

347

Question:
One of the best things you can hope for after whacking a ball with a stick.
Answer:
Homerun

Question:
This patch of land stands alone.
Answer:
Island

Question:
Securing your documents is easy with these trusty metal objects.
Answer:
Staples

Question:
These sucks.
Answer:
Vacuum

Question:
If you're on a diet, smelling a fresh pan of brownies could be described at this.
Answer:
Torture

Question:
This man has an obsession with spinach.
Answer:
Popeye

Question:
What you do to determine the length of something.
Answer:
Measure

Question:
These are great fun until you realize you don't have all the pieces.
Answer:
Puzzle

Question:
Scottish knee-length formal wear for men.
Answer:
Kilt

Question:
When life gives you these, make a refreshing beverage.
Answer:
Lemon

Question:
This has been cut with water
Answer:
Diluted

Question:
Some are clean and some are dirty, but all are meant to get a chuckle.
Answer:
Jokes

Question:
You throw away the outside and cook the inside. You then eat the outside and throw away the inside.
Answer:
Corn

Question:
Known to accessorize with feathers, trumpets, and harps.
Answer:
Angels

Question:

Answer:

Question:
Which letter of the alphabet has the most water?
Answer:
C

Question:
What kind of dog keeps the best time?
Answer:
Watchdog

Question:
What time of day, when written in a capital letters, is the same forwards, backwards and upside down?
Answer:

Question:
Laughing Out
Answer:
Loud

Question:
A tasty reward given to well behaved dogs and kids
Answer:
Treat

Question:
A caribbean shape that makes ships disappear
Answer:
Triangle

Question:
It takes two people to do this
Answer:
Tango

Question:
What has a face and two hands but no arms or legs?
Answer:
Clock

Question:
What five-letter word becomes shorter when you add two letters to it?
Answer:

Question:
What word begins and ends with an 'E' but only has one letter?
Answer:
Envelope

Question:
What has a neck but no head?
Answer:
Bottle

Question:
What type of cheese is made backwards?
Answer:
Edam

Question:
What gets wetter as it dries?
Answer:
Towel

Question:
Which letter of the alphabet has the most water?
Answer:
C

Question:
What starts with a 'P', ends with an 'E' and has thousands of letters?
Answer:

Question:
What has to be broken before you can eat it?
Answer:
Egg

Question:
What begins with T, ends with T and has T in it?
Answer:
Teapot

Question:
Teddy bears are never hungry because they are always what?
Answer:
Stuffed

Question:
What belongs to you but others use it more than you do?
Answer:
Name

Question:
The more you take aways, the larger it becomes? What is it?
Answer:
Hole

Question:
What is full of holes, but can still hold a lot of water?
Answer:

Sponge

Question:
Where do fish keep their money?
Answer:
Riverbank

Question:
What do you get when you cross an automobile with a household animal?
Answer:
Carpet

Question:
Mary's father has 4 children; three are named Nana, Nene, and Nini. So what is the 4th child's name?
Answer:
Mary

Question:
What bone has a sense of humor?
Answer:
Humorous

Question:
The more of them you take, the more you leave behind. What are they?
Answer:
Footsteps

Question:
What is that you will break everytime you name it?

RIDDLE BOOK FOR KIDS

354

Answer:
Silence

Question:
What has four fingers and one thumb, but is not alive?
Answer:
Glove

Question:
What flies without wings?
Answer:
Time

Question:
What turns everything around, but does not move?
Answer:
Mirror

Question:
What is half of two plus two?
Answer:
Three

Question:
What word looks the same upside down and backwards?
Answer:
Swims

Question:
What kind of fish chases a mouse?

Answer:
Catfish

Question:
Your mother's brother's only brother-in-law is asleep on your coach. Who is asleep on your couch?
Answer:
Dad

Question:
What's the difference between here and there?
Answer:
T

Question:
What goes up and down without moving?
Answer:
Stairs

Question:
Take off my skin and I won't cry, but you will, What am I?
Answer:
Onion

Question:
What doesn't get any wetter, no matter how much rain falls on it?
Answer:
Water

Question:

What sits in a corner while traveling all around the world?   356
Answer:
Stamp

Question:
I have a face, two arms, and two hands, yet I can not move. I count to twelve, yet I can not speak. I can still tell you something everyday.
Answer:
Clock

Question:
You enter a dark room. You have only one match. There is an oil lamp, a furnace, and a stove in the room. Which would you light first?
Answer:
Match

Question:
What is round on both ends and hi in the middle?
Answer:
Ohio

Question:
What do you call a dog that sweats so much?
Answer:
Hotdog

Question:
What do you call a rabbit with fleas?
Answer:
Bugs Bunny

Question:
What rains at the north pole?
Answer:
Reindeer

Question:
What kind of apple has a short temper?
Answer:
Crabapple

Question:
What do you do with a dead chemist?
Answer:
Barium

Question:
What calls for help, when written in capital letters, is the same forwards,
backwards and upside down?
Answer:
SOS

Question:
What body part is pronounced as one letter but written with three, only
two different letters are used?
Answer:
Eye

Question:
What is 2+2? What is 4+4? What is 8+8? What is 16+16? Pick a number
between 12 and 5

Answer:
Seven

Question:
Feed me and I live, give me something to drink and i'll die, What am I?
Answer:
Fire

Question:
What keeps things green and keeps kids occupied in the summertime?
Answer:
Sprinkler

Question:
Old Mcdonald had this
Answer:
Farm

Question:
Poorly behaved children often find themselves sitting in these
Answer:
Corner

Question:
Brings you may flowers
Answer:
Showers

Question:
A shower that lights up the sky

Answer:
Meteor

Question:
Longer than a decade and shorter than a milennium
Answer:
Century

Question:
Rolling on floor
Answer:
Laughing

Question:
Rabbits do this to carrots and Jason Mraz does this to ears
Answer:
Nibble

Question:
These minerals are vital to your health
Answer:
Vitamin

Question:
Commits friendly home invasions one night a year
Answer:
Santa claus

Question:
Treats said to be based on a shephero's staff

Answer:
Candy cane

Question:
Everyone claims to know a way to stop these involuntary contractions but none of them work
Answer:
Hiccup

Question:
Has 4 lucky leaves
Answer:
Shamrock

Question:
One of the best things you can hope for after whacking a ball with a stick
Answer:
Home run

Question:
They put the heat in pop tarts
Answer:
Toaster

Question:
What has a ring, but no finger?
Answer:
Telephone

Question:

361 What has four legs, but can't walk?
Answer:
Table

Question:
What is higher without the head, than with it?
Answer:
Pillow

Question:
What is harder to catch the faster you run?
Answer:
Breath

Question:
What invention lets you look right through a wall?
Answer:
Window

Question:
What is that you will break everytime you name it?
Answer:
Silence

Question:
What is made of wood, but can't be sawed?
Answer:
Sawdust

Question:

What is a witch's favorite school subject?
Answer:
Spelling

Question:
What is an aliens favourite sport?
Answer:
Spaceball

Question:
What is the saddest fruit?
Answer:
Blueberry

Question:
What is black and white and read all over?
Answer:
Newspaper

Question:
What is easy to get into, and hard to get out of?
Answer:
Trouble

Question:
What is there more of the less you see?
Answer:
Darkness

Question:

368 If two hours ago, it was as long after one o'clock in the afternoon as it was before one o'clock in the morning, what time would it be now?
Answer:
Nine

Question:
What is as big as you are and yet does not weigh anything?
Answer:
Shadow

Question:
What types of words are these: Madam, Civic, Eye, Level?
Answer:
Palindrome

Question:
When you have me, you feel like sharing me. But, if you do share me, you don't have me. What am I?
Answer:
Secret

Question:
The person who makes it has no need for it. The person who purchases it does not use it. The person who does use it does not know he or she is. What is it?
Answer:
Coffin

Question:
It is an insect, and the first part of its name is the name of another insect.

What is it?
Answer:
Beetle

Question:
What english word retains the same pronunciation, even after you take away four of its five letters?
Answer:
Queue

Question:
What becomes white when it is dirty?
Answer:
Blackboard

Question:
What word of five letters has only one left when two letters are removed?
Answer:
Stone

Question:
How many 9 s are there between 1 and 100?
Answer:
Twenty

Question:
Which vehicle is spelled the same forwards and backwards?
Answer:
Racecar

Question:
I am lighter than air but a million men cannot lift me up, What am I?
Answer:
Bubble

Question:
Five men were eating apples, a finished before B, but behind C. D finished before E, but behind B. What was the finishing order?
Answer:
CABDE

Question:
David's father has three sons: Snap, Crackle, and ?
Answer:
David

Question:
It is everything to someone, and nothing to everyone else. What is it?
Answer:
Mind

Question:
What has a mouth but can't chew?
Answer:
River

Question:
A man says,"Brothers and sisters, have I none, but that man's father is my father's son." Who is he pointing at?
Answer:

Question:
If it is two hours later, then it will take half as much time till it's midnight as it would be if it were an hour later. What time is it?
Answer:
Nine

Question:
Forward I am heavy, backwards I am not. What am I?
Answer:
Ton

Question:
What object has keys that open no locks, space but no room, and you can enter but not go in?
Answer:
Keyboard

Question:
Some try to hide, some try to cheat, but time will show, we always will meet, try as you might, to guess my name, I promise you'll know, when you I do claim.
Answer:
Death

Question:
First you see me in the grass dressed in yellow gay; next I am in dainty white, then I fly away. What am I?
Answer:

Question:
Hands she has but does not hold, teeth she has but does not bite, feet she has but they are cold, eyes she has but without sight. Who is she?
Answer:
Doll

Question:
What lies in bed, and stands in bed, first white then red. The plumber it gets, the better the old woman likes it?
Answer:
Strawberry

Question:
Inside a burning house, this thing is best to make. And best to make it quickly, before the fire's too much to take!
Answer:
Haste

Question:
What can bring back the dead; make us cry, make us laugh, make us young; born in an instant yet lasts a life time?
Answer:
Memories

Question:
An openended barrel, I am shaped like a hive. I am filled with the flesh, and the flesh is alive! What am I?
Answer:

Question:
Violet, indigo, blue and green, yellow, orange and red; these are the colors you have seen after the storm has fled. What am I?
Answer:
Rainbow

Question:
I was carried into a dark room, and set on fire. I wept, and then my head was cut off. What am I?
Answer:
Candle

Question:
What does no man want, yet no man want to lose?
Answer:
Job

Question:
This old one runs forever, but never moves at all. He has not lungs nor throat, but still a mighty roaring call. What is it?
Answer:
Waterfall

Question:
Mountains will crumble and temples will fall, and no man can survive its endless call. What is it?
Answer:
Time

369

Question:
What can go up a chimney down, but cannot go down a chimney up?
Answer:
Umbrella

Question:
I pass before the sun, yet make no shadow. What am I?
Answer:
Wind

Question:
When they are caught, they are thrown away. When they escape, you itch all day. What are they?
Answer:
Fleas

Question:
You can spin, wheel and twist, but this thing can turn without moving. What is it?
Answer:
Milk

Question:
Never resting, never still. Moving silently from hill to hill. It does not walk, run or trot. All is cool where it is not.
Answer:
Sunshine

Question:
Different lights do make me strange, thus into different sizes I will

change.
Answer:
Pupil

Question:
When asked how old she was, suzie replied, "in two years I will be twice as old as I was five years ago." How old is she?
Answer:
Twelve

Question:
I have two arms, but fingers none. I have two feet, but cannot run. I carry well, but I have found I carry best with my feet off the ground. What am I?
Answer:
Wheelbarrow

Question:
What has a tongue, cannot walk, but gets around a lot?
Answer:
Shoe

Question:
What has feet and legs, and nothing else?
Answer:
Stockings

Question:
What has no beginning, end, or middle?
Answer:
Doughnut

371

Question:
What do you throw out when you want to use it, but take in when you don't want to use it?
Answer:
Anchor

Question:
You hear it speak, for it has a hard tongue. But it cannot breathe, for it has not a lung. What is it?
Answer:
Bell

Question:
What is that which goes with a car, comes with a car, is of no use to a car, and yet the car cannot go without it?
Answer:
Noise

Question:
What is big and yellow and comes in the morning, to brigten mom's day?
Answer:
School Bus

Question:
You are in a room with 3 monkeys. One monkey has a banana, one has a stick, and one has nothing. Who is the smartest primate?
Answer:
You

Question:

I'm the part of the bird that's not in the sky. I can swim in the ocean and
yet remain dry. What am I?
Answer:
Shadow

Question:
If you were standing directly on antarcticas south pole facing north,
which direction would you travel if you took one step backward?
Answer:
North

Question:
Look at me. I can bring a smile to your face, a tear to your eye, or even a
thought to your mind. But, I can't be seen. What am I?
Answer:
Memories

Question:
When the day after tomorrow is yesterday, today will be as far from
wednesday as today was from wednesday when the day before yesterday
was tomorrow. What is the day after this day?
Answer:
Thursday

Question:
Who spends the day at the window, goes to the table for meals and hides
at night?
Answer:
Fly

373

Question:
In a tunnel of darksness lies a beast of iron. It can only attack when pulled back. What is it?
Answer:
Bullet

Question:
What is easy to get into, but hard to get out of?
Answer:
Trouble

Question:
Lives without a body, hears without ears, speaks without a mouth, to which the air alone gives birth. What is it?
Answer:
Echo

Question:
Three lives have i. Gentle enough to soothe the skin. Light enough to caress the sky. Hard enough to crack rocks. What am I?
Answer:
Water

Question:
I go in hard. I come out soft. You blow me hard. What am I?
Answer:
Gum

Question:
What is it that no man ever yet did see, which never was, but always is to

be?
Answer:
Tomorrow

Question:
I am in the sky but also in the ground. When you study me, no matter how long, I will always end with an f. I may be in your yard but not in your house. What am I?
Answer:
Leaf

Question:
What I am visible to you, you cannot see me, but when I am invisible, you long to see me. I am plenty with someone patient, but all the more scarce with a hasty one. I am greater than all, but still in the control of those who value my existence. Who am i?
Answer:
Time

Question:
I cover what's real; hide what is true, but sometimes bring out the courage in you. What am I?
Answer:
Makeup

Question:
Mountains will crumble and temples will fall, and no man can survive its endless call. What is it?
Answer:
Time

375

Question:
What is black when you buy it, red when you use it, and gray when you throw it away?
Answer:
Charcoal

Question:
Though liquid in nature, don't push me too far for then I will break, and the damage may scar. What am I?
Answer:
Glass

Question:
Before Mt. Everest Was discovered as the highest mountain in the world, which mountain was the highest?
Answer:
Mt Everest

Question:
Answer:

Question:
They come out at night without being called, and are lost in the day without being stolen. What are they?
Answer:
Stars

Question:
It is something you will never see again.
Answer:

Question:
What goes round the house and in the house but never touches the house?
Answer:
Sun

Question:
What is it that you can keep after giving it to someone else?
Answer:
Your Word

Question:
What goes up and down without moving?
Answer:
Stairs

Question:
When one does not know what it is, then it is something; but when one knows what it is, then it is nothing.
Answer:
Riddle

Question:
I bind it and it walks. I loose it and it stops.
Answer:
Sandal

Question:

37 Lives without a body, hears without ears, speaks without a mouth, to which the air alone gives birth.

Answer:

Echo

Question:

What is put on a table, cut, but never eaten?

Answer:

Cards

Question:

What belongs to you but others use it more than you do?

Answer:

Your Name

Question:

Has four legs, but is not alive.

Answer:

Chair

Question:

What has a neck but no head, and wears a cap?

Answer:

Bottle

Question:

What has a tongue, cannot walk, but gets around a lot?

Answer:

Shoe

Question:

It flies without wings.

Answer:

Time

Question:

What gets beaten, and whipped, but never cries?

Answer:

Egg

Question:

What has a ring but no fingers?

Answer:

Telephone

Question:

What is made of wood, but can't be sawed?

Answer:

Sawdust

Question:

How many letters are in the alphabet?

Answer:

Eleven

Question:

Who prefers to travel on vines and pal around with gorillas?

Answer:

Tarzan

Question:
It is a tasty reward that is given to well behaved dogs and kids.
Answer:
Treat

Question:
Take off my skin - I won't cry, but you will! What am I?
Answer:
Onion

Question:
Something very helpful if you want to go gently down a stream.
Answer:
Rowboat

Question:
It is something you make after you've weighed your options.
Answer:
Decision

Question:
John's mom had three children. The first child was april. The second child was May. What was the third Child's name?
Answer:
John

Question:
You have three stoves: A gas stove, a wood stove, and a coal stove, but only one match. Which should you light first?
Answer:

Question:
I am but three holes. When you come out of me, you are still inside me.
What am I?
Answer:
Shirt

Question:
What do you have when you're sitting down that you don't have when you're standing up?
Answer:
Lap

Question:
The favorite beverage of friendly polar bears as shown in the ads.
Answer:
Coke

Question:
What do you call a lonely patch of land?
Answer:
Island

Question:
The coziest place for Dracula.
Answer:
Coffin

Question:

What is used to yell in a text?
Answer:
Caps

Question:
It is a common and favored clothing material among biker gangs and superheroes.
Answer:
Leather

Question:
A type of hammer that brings a room to order.
Answer:
Gavel

Question:
People in love are often bound to this.
Answer:
Married

Question:
It is the assumed nocturnal symbol of Mr. Wayne. What is it?
Answer:
Bat

Question:
What is black and white and read all over?
Answer:
Newspaper

Question:
A kind of shower that lighten up the sky.
Answer:
Meteor

Question:
Both old people and owls are said to be possessing this trait.
Answer:
Wise

Question:
He has married many women, but has never been married. Who is he?
Answer:
Preacher

Question:
These are knee-length formal wear for men popular in the highlands.
Answer:
Kilt

Question:
This is where the wind comes sweeping down the plain. Not to mention
the waving wheat.
Answer:
Oklahoma

Question:
It is a seasonal yet regular fashion trend which is named after the type of
weather its worn in.
Answer:

Question:
All about, but cannot be seen. Can be captured, cannot be held. No Throat, but can be heard. What is it?
Answer:
Wind

Question:
It can be done to buttons and shopping carts. What is it?
Answer:
Push

Question:
He is the kind of person who has powers to save the day.
Answer:
Superman

Question:
This is a natural tattoo on babies.
Answer:
Birthmark

Question:
A cat-like name for those of the left handed persuasion which is very common in boxing.
Answer:
Southpaw

Question:

385This is your stomach's way of letting you know you've neglected it.
Answer:
Grumble

Question:
They are the shore's gallant knights.
Answer:
Coast Guard

Question:
It is the great nemesis of the lactose intolerant
Answer:
Dairy

Question:
What goes round and round the wood but never goes into the wood?
Answer:
Bark

Question:
Schwarzenegger has a big one, Michael J. Fox's is small, Madonna doesn't have one, the pope doesn't use his, and Cliton uses his all the time.
Answer:
Last Name

Question:
Never ahead, ever behind, yet flying swiftly past. For a child, I last forever, for adults, I'm gone too fast. What am I?
Answer:
Youth

Question:
It could make arrows fly and kites soar. What is it?
Answer:
String

Question:
I am taken from a mine, and shut up in a wooden case, from which I am never released, and yet I am used by almost everybody.
Answer:
Pencil Lead

Question:
The profession of both Jimi Hendrix and Eric Clapton
Answer:
Guitarist

Question:
The thinkers usually hold this body part.
Answer:
Chin

Question:
This both describes gorgeous woman and an excellent punch.
Answer:
Knockout

Question:
This is something you carry while singing.
Answer:
Tune

Question:
When set loose, I fly away. Never so cursed, as when I go astray. What am I?
Answer:
Fart

Question:
What is Santa's favorite entrance for home invasion?
Answer:
Chimney

Question:
The plant that is responsible for spreading a lot of gossip.
Answer:
Grapevine

Question:
It is basically a cake made of cow.
Answer:
Meatloaf

Question:
It is the transportation of choice for princesses to attend balls.
Answer:
Carriage

Question:
John Lennon once sang about being this toothy creature. What is it?
Answer:
Walrus

Question:
This is a plant named after a light source. What is it?
Answer:
Sunflower

Question:
It does hurt when it breaks and if it stops, you are dead.
Answer:
Heart

Question:
Some are clean and some are dirty, but all are meant to get a chuckle.
Most like it, some takes offense from it.
Answer:
Joke

Question:
Other terms for this handy device include hoohicky, doo-dad and
watchyamacallit. Some people are so addicted to this.
Answer:
Gadget

Question:
It is the most common hour to have a gunfight in a western scene.
Answer:
Noon

Question:
Sport Olympians use this to get high jump up in the air.
Answer:

Question:
It is one more than a duet.
Answer:
Trio

Question:
This is the common vehicle both George J. Jetson and Neil A. Armstrong drove to work.
Answer:
Spaceship

Question:
They are the most foreign visitors you could ever imagine.
Answer:
Alien

Question:
Answer:

Question:
This heavy and ancient suit was not worn with a tie, but was always worn in battle.
Answer:
Armor

Question:
What has a hundred limbs, sometimes leaves, but cannot walk?
Answer:

Question:
When you find this in a road, you will not use it to eat, but will be forced to make a decision.
Answer:
Fork

Question:
What invention lets you look right through a wall?
Answer:
Window

Question:
Those with eyes bigger than their stomach will definitely leave the restaurant with one of them. It is named after a house pet as well.
Answer:
Doggy Bag

Question:
A close relative of ketchup that people often spread on their dog.
Answer:
Mustard

Question:
If you drop a yellow hat in the red sea what does it become?
Answer:
Wet

Question:

391   I jump when I walk and I sit where I stand. What am I?

Answer:

Kangaroo

Question:

He is known to commit a friendly home invasion one night a year, never taking but always leaving stuff behind.

Answer:

Santa Claus

Question:

The more of me there is, the less you see.

Answer:

Darkness

Question:

Often wandering the streets, this group of people cannot afford to be choosers.

Answer:

Beggars

Question:

What holds water yet is full of holes?

Answer:

Sponge

Question:

The state of holding a person within a person or an animal within an animal?

Answer:

Question:
Feared on the playground, he steals your lunch money and distributes wedgies.
Answer:
Bully

Question:
What is brown, has a head and a tail. But no legs?
Answer:
Penny

Question:
I'm the part of the bird that's not in the sky. I can swim in the ocean and yet remain dry. What am I?
Answer:
Shadow

Question:
It's been around for millions of years, but it's no more than a month old. What is it?
Answer:
Moon

Question:
The more you take, the more you leave behind. They vary in size. What are they?
Answer:
Footprints

393

Question:
I engulf you in darkness but you see many things. I can be resisted but a lack of me leaves rings. What am I?
Answer:
Sleep

Question:
I'm a container with the inside golden that can't be opened unless I'm broken. What am I?
Answer:
Egg

Question:
Which vehicle is spelled the same forwards and backwards?
Answer:
Racecar

Question:
What kind of coat can be put on only when wet?
Answer:
Paint

Question:
What goes around the world but stays in a corner?
Answer:
Stamp

Question:
I can be cracked, I can be made. I can be told and I can be played.
Answer:

Question:
What loses its head every morning and gets it back every night?
Answer:
Pillow

Question:
What starts with a 'p' ends with an 'e' and has thousands of letters?
Answer:
Post Office

Question:
I have married many women but I am not married. Who am I?
Answer:
Priest

Question:
What is it that you ought to keep after you have given it to someone else?
Answer:
Promise

Question:
What is red and blue, purple and green? No one can reach it, not even the queen.
Answer:
Rainbow

Question:
When you know me, I am nothing. What you don't know me, I am some-

thing. What am I?
Answer:
Riddle

Question:
What English word retains the same pronunciation, even after you take away four of its five letters?
Answer:
Queue

Question:
Which word in the English language becomes shorter when it is lengthened?
Answer:
Short

Question:
As your ideas grow, I shrink. What am I?
Answer:
Pencil

Question:
A certain crime is punishable if attempted. But not punishable if committed. What is it?
Answer:
Suicide

Question:
What demands an answer, but asks no questions?
Answer:

Question:
I make noise yet you don't see me make it. I alarm for good yet sometimes for worse. I have a companion. What am I?
Answer:
Thunder

Question:
Forwards, I'm heavy. Backwards, I'm not. What am I?
Answer:
Ton

Question:
I am everywhere. I am inside you. I surround you. I can be seen by you. I can kill you. Yet you play in me. What am I?
Answer:
Water

Question:
I can alter the actions of a king and leave puzzled the greatest of philosophers. What am I?
Answer:
Woman

Question:
What goes up and never comes down and affects people?
Answer:
Age

397

Question:
Everybody has some. You can lose some, you can gain some. But you cannot live without it. What am I?
Answer:
Blood

Question:
What English word has three consecutive double letters?
Answer:
Bookkeeper

Question:
I am as light as a feather, yet no man can hold me for long. What am I?
Answer:
Breath

Question:
I fly but have no wings. I cry but have no eyes. I see the sky get dark and I see when the sun comes up. What am I?
Answer:
Cloud

Question:
The man who invented it doesn't want it. The man who bought it doesn't need it. The man who needs it doesn't know it. What is it?
Answer:
Coffin

Question:
Hands she has but does not hold, teeth she has but does not bite, feet she

has but they are cold, eyes she has but without sight.
Answer:
Doll

Question:
I have no beginning, end, or middle. What am I?
Answer:
Doughnut

Question:
You heard me before, yet you hear me again. Then I die, 'til you call me again. What am I?
Answer:
Echo

Question:
What starts with the letter T, is filled with T and ends in T?
Answer:
Teapot

Question:
What is so delicate that saying its name breaks it?
Answer:
Silence

Question:
What is always coming but never arrives?
Answer:
Tomorrow

399

Question:
What goes through towns and over hills but never moves?
Answer:
Road

Question:
What has a head but never weeps, has a bed but never sleeps, can run but never walks, and has a bank but no money?
Answer:
River

Question:
The more it dries, the wetter it becomes. What is it?
Answer:
Towel

Question:
It is the electronic version of junk mail or a salty meat in a can
Answer:
Spam

Question:
It is an aquatic creature whose name is rather "Tight"
Answer:
Seal

Question:
The famous royal young lady who had several short men following her.
Answer:
Snow White

Question:
It is filthy place that serves as a home to a grouchy green puppet.
Answer:
Trash Can

Question:
They are known for their natural tuxedos and marching
Answer:
Penguins

Question:
What has 2 banks, but no money?
Answer:
River

Question:
Has four legs, but is not alive.
Answer:
Chair

Question:
What keeps things green and keeps the kids occupied in the summer time?
Answer:
Sprinkler

Question:
Round as a button, deep as a well. If you want me to talk, you must first pull my tail. What am I?
Answer:

Question:
It is a sleep-inducing melody.
Answer:
Lullaby

Question:
It is a storage facility for criminals and fire-breathing reptiles.
Answer:
Dungeon

Question:
To be one of them, you need special abilities and brightly colored under-
wear.
Answer:
Superhero

Question:
Not my sister nor my brother but still the child of my mother and father.
Who am I?
Answer:
Myself

Question:
They have not flesh, nor feathers, nor scales, nor bone. Yet they have fin-
gers and thumbs of their own. What are they?
Answer:
Gloves

403

Question:
It is something that is often sold by child entrepreneurs during summer.
Answer:
Lemonade

Question:
The most popular itsy bitsy teeny weeny yellow polka dot variety.
Answer:
Bikini

Question:
It is longer than a decade and shorter than a millennium.
Answer:
Century

Question:
What is long and slim, works in light; has but one eye, and an awful bite?
Answer:
Needle

Question:
I have two heads but only one body. The stiller I stand, the faster I run.
What am I?
Answer:
Hourglass

Question:
Lighter than what I am made of. More of me is hidden than seen. What am I?
Answer:

Question:
What kind of tree can you carry in your hand?
Answer:
Palm

Question:
With no hammer or any kind of tool I build my house so quickly. What am I?
Answer:
Spider

Question:
It is where everyone wants to run home and stealing is encouraged.
Answer:
Baseball

Question:
What fuels backyard get-togethers?
Answer:
Charcoal

Question:
What kind of noise does Santa's reindeers make?
Answer:
Jingle

Question:
Where on earth do the ways always blow from the south?

405

Answer:
North Pole

Question:
I run distances, often making many turns, yet I never move one foot.
What am I?
Answer:
Watch

Question:
What can go up a chimney down, but cannot go down a chimney up?
Answer:
Umbrella

Question:
What is it that when you take away the whole, you still have some left over.
Answer:
Wholesome

Question:
What goes up and down the stairs without moving?
Answer:
Carpet

Question:
What goes into the water black and come out red?
Answer:
Lobster

Question:

You do not want to have it, but when you do have it, you do not want to lose it. What is it?

Answer:

Lawsuit

Question:

If I drink, I die. If I eat, I am fine. What am I?

Answer:

Fire

Question:

What has 4 eyes but can't see?

Answer:

Mississippi

Question:

I'm tall when I'm young and I'm short when I'm old. What am I?

Answer:

Candle

Question:

What gets broken without being held?

Answer:

Promise

Question:

Who can only prevent forest fires?

Answer:

Smokey

Question:
What company makes billions of dollars selling windows?
Answer:
Microsoft

Question:
What do you call a greedy grumpy holiday hater?
Answer:
Scrooge

Question:
A kind of game with love and service played by singles and pairs.
Answer:
Tennis

Question:
It has a face and two hands but no arms or legs. What is this?
Answer:
Clock

Question:
A place where the titanic is still chilling.
Answer:
Atlantic

Question:
It can be found at the back of a book or in an abdomen.
Answer:
Appendix

Question:
What is the delicious way of presenting numbers?
Answer:
Pie Chart

Question:
I turn around once. What is out will not get in. I turn around again. What is in will not get out. What am I?
Answer:
Key

Question:
I have an end but no beginning, a home but no family, a space without room. I never speak but there is no word I cannot make. What am I?
Answer:
Keyboard

Question:
You eat something you neither plant nor plow. It is the son of water, but if water touches it. It dies. What is it?
Answer:
Salt

Question:
What is the center of gravity?
Answer:
V

Question:
What has a mouth but can't chew?

Answer:
River

Question:
How many letters are in the alphabet?
Answer:
Eleven

Question:
If you have me, you want to share me. If you share me, you haven't got me. What am I?
Answer:
Secret

Question:
A common need for both courage and hardcover for books.
Answer:
Spine

Question:
If rabbits do this to carrots, Jason Mraz does this to ears. What is this?
Answer:
Nibble

Question:
You get these directions from outer space.
Answer:
GPS

Question:

They are toothy nocturnal immortals.

Answer:

Vampire

Question:

It brings celebrities closer into your home every now and then.

Answer:

Television

Question:

Thousands of these come together to make an amazing digital image.

Answer:

Pixel

Question:

What animal dwells in water and best known for its work ethic?

Answer:

Beaver

Question:

It is a popular afterlife destination where you want to send people when you're mad at them.

Answer:

Hell

Question:

It is carried by both mad bats and dogs. What is this?

Answer:

Rabies

411

Question:
What screams when put in a pot of boiling water?
Answer:
Lobster

Question:
What is an acceptable act of violence during saint Patrick's day?
Answer:
Pinch

Question:
I am the killer of trees but people need me. I can be blown away by a breeze and I have been here since ancient Greece. What am I?
Answer:
Paper

Question:
What is harder to catch the faster you run?
Answer:
Your Breath

Question:
Which word in the dictionary is spelled incorrectly?
Answer:
Incorrectly

Question:
What word , when written in capital letters, is the same forwards, backwards, and upside down?
Answer:

Question:
What doesn't exist, but has a name?
Answer:
Nothing

Question:
Two legs I have, and this will confound: Only at rest do they touch the ground! What am I?
Answer:
Wheelbarrow

Question:
Has a foot on each side and one in the middle.
Answer:
Yardstick

Question:
What do you call the offspring of a feline and a Xerox machine?
Answer:
Copycat

Question:
This old one runs forever, but never moves at all. He has not lungs nor throat, but still a mighty roaring call. What is it?
Answer:
Waterfall

Question:

414

Glittering points that downward thrust, sparkling spears that never rust.
What is it?
Answer:
Icicle

Question:
What 7 letter word becomes longer when the third letter is removed?
Answer:
Lounger

Question:
You must keep this thing, its loss will affect your brothers. For once yours is lost, it will soon be lost by others. What is it?
Answer:
Temper

Question:
My tines be long, my tines be short. My tines end ere, my first report.
What am I?
Answer:
Lightning

Question:
A skin have I, more eyes than one. I can be very nice when I am done.
What am I?
Answer:
Potato

Question:
What makes leaping off a bridge fun?

Answer:
Bungee

Question:
When a doctor hits you with a hammer he is testing you this.
Answer:
Reflex

Question:
What gets whiter the dirtier that it gets?
Answer:
Chalkboard

Question:
I drive men mad for the love of me. Easily beaten, never free. What am I?
Answer:
Gold

Question:
Something that is handy when you need to measure something or run a kingdom.
Answer:
Ruler

Question:
These are crisp, green, and are found near deli sandwiches.
Answer:
Pickle

Question:

415   It is a monkey food that makes people slip and fall in cartoons.
Answer:
Bananas

Question:
It can be heard in a court or used to carry briefs.
Answer:
Case

Question:
It is something that is owned by old McDonald.
Answer:
Farm

Question:
The one fashion accessory both farmers and hipsters love.
Answer:
Suspenders

Question:
Who is the father of Mickey Mouse?
Answer:
Walt Disney

Question:
It happens when something has been cut with H2O
Answer:
Diluted

Question:

This is the drinkable phase of matter.
Answer:
Liquid

Question:
A colorful cuisine without flesh.
Answer:
Vegetable

Question:
He may seem to work in public transportation but he actually works in a restaurant.
Answer:
Busboy

Question:
It is the offspring of a circle and a rectangle
Answer:
Oval

Question:
It is the surname of Cinderella's love.
Answer:
Charming

Question:
Lovely and round, I shine with pale light. Grown in the darkness, a lady's delight. What am I?
Answer:
Pearls

417

Question:
Both boats with holes and dirty dishes have this in common.
Answer:
Sink

Question:
Children who misbehave often find themselves sitting in this area.
Answer:
Corners

Question:
It flavors your food and divides the year up. What is it?
Answer:
Season

Question:
It is a desert oasis where money magically appears or disappears from your pocket.
Answer:
Las Vegas

Question:
It could be a tangly game but can also become a destructive weather phenomenon.
Answer:
Twister

Question:
If you are a sore loser, you are often called the sour variety of this fruit.
Answer:

Question:
It brings the sky and the stars a lot closer.
Answer:
Telescope

Question:
What goes from new York to California without ever moving?
Answer:
Highway

Question:
What is it that Indiana jones likes to crack?
Answer:
Whip

Question:
This type of tempting cuisine is independent of utensils and usually tastes better than it sounds.
Answer:
Finger Food

Question:
It is probably the most laid-back member of the animal kingdom.
Answer:
Sloth

Question:
Remove six letters from this sequence to reveal a familiar English word -

BSAINXLEATNTEARS
Answer:
Bananas

Question:
I have seas without water. I have forests without wood. I have deserts without sand. I have houses with no bricks.
Answer:
Map

Question:
How many times can you subtract the number 5 from 25?
Answer:
One

Question:
All about, but cannot be seen. Can be captured, cannot be held. No throat, but can be heard.
Answer:
Wind

Question:
It is sometimes known to have silver linings.
Answer:
Cloud

Question:
It is a form of plastic money.
Answer:
Credit Card

Question:

Kids loves to hunt for them and adults make sure they are not all in one basket.

Answer:

Eggs

Question:

I stink when living and smell good when dead?

Answer:

Bacon

Question:

If there are three cups of sugar and you take one away, how many do you have?

Answer:

One

Question:

I am full of wisdom and knowledge. I get what you want in a blink of an eye. I am known to man as full of endless wisdom. What am I?

Answer:

Computer

Question:

A great mysterious place that the bold have been known to journey into.

Answer:

Unknown

Question:

The only pet who lived in a town where an inordinate number of children

fell down wells.
Answer:
Lassie

Question:
If life gets tough, what do you have that you can always count on?
Answer:
Fingers

Question:
What comes down but never goes up and happens most often in the spring?
Answer:
Rain

Question:
Spies and detectives do this to phones and musical shoes make this sound.
Answer:
Tap

Question:
This is the most famous bank where children keep their assets.
Answer:
Piggy Bank

Question:
Environmentalists really want to keep this area from drying.
Answer:
Wetland

Question:
These are believed to be found at the end of rainbows.
Answer:
Pots

Question:
If a man carried my burden he would break his back. I am not rich, but leave silver in my track. What am I?
Answer:
Snail

Question:
A common place to find can-can girls and drunk cowboys. What place is this?
Answer:
Saloon

Question:
She is covered in dust and is always jealous.
Answer:
Tinker Bell

Question:
The fans of the pied piper's smooth sound who are feared by elephants.
Answer:
Mice

Question:
They are the group who manages the winged engines of war.
Answer:

Air Force

Question:
If you happen to possess two left feet, this profession will probably rule out of your prospects.
Answer:
Dancer

Question:
This is often found in doctor's offices and a common sight in pirate flags.
Answer:
Skeleton

Question:
This became a fashion statement in the garden of Eden.
Answer:
Fig Leaf

Question:
I known a word of letters three. Add two, and fewer there will be.
Answer:
Few

Question:
What do you call the edge of both earth and bread?
Answer:
Crust

Question:
It is a gruesome form of betray.

Answer:
Backstab

Question:
Those ambitious people will climb the social version of this contraption.
What is this?
Answer:
Ladder

Question:
Both peaches and a certain couture have this in common.
Answer:
Juicy

Question:
This can be found under bridges and even on the internet.
Answer:
Troll

Question:
This is the known hairdo for nascar fans.
Answer:
Mullet

Question:
It can be used onstage or to express admiration. What is it?
Answer:
Props

Question:

425 They are producers of pies and burgers and are great for tipping.
Answer:
Cows

Question:
It can cause deflation of tires when dropped from the rear of spy cars.
Answer:
Spikes

Question:
Possibly the only famous plumber who has the courage to ever to rescue a princess.
Answer:
Mario

Question:
Sources in Hollywood state that the men of this ancient city wore leather speedos and waxed their chests.
Answer:
Sparta

Question:
She is fred and Wilma's child who is named after a stone.
Answer:
Pebbles

Question:
Some people are conscious enough to count these while some just consume them.
Answer:

Question:
Weight in my belly, trees on my back. Nails in my ribs, feet I do lack. What am I?
Answer:
Ship

Question:
They're actually great swimmers now, but later they will become excellent hoppers.
Answer:
Tadpole

Question:
They do look like a hippo crossed with a unicorn. What are they?
Answer:
Rhino

Question:
This is a single seater best accompanied by circus music coupled with a great balance.
Answer:
Unicycle

Question:
What is round on both sides but high in the middle?
Answer:
Ohio

RIDDLE BOOK FOR KIDS

Question:
It has 88 keys, but none of these will open a door.
Answer:
Piano

Question:
What animal gives away money and says moo?
Answer:
Cash Cow

Question:
This comes in a tin can and are best known to cure halitosis.
Answer:
Altoids

Question:
It is good for telling the future or racking up in a game.
Answer:
Eight Ball

Question:
Long ago, dragons are believed to do this to their gold.
Answer:
Hoard

Question:
If you happen to wake up at dawn, you'll probably find this covering the lawn.
Answer:
Dew

429

Question:
People like this usually live in rural areas, unless they are lucky enough to strike oil and move to Beverly hills.
Answer:
Hillbilly

Question:
Both cockroaches and illegal drug laboratories or syndicates do fear this.
Answer:
Raid

Question:
You will have this response if you would go salivating at the mention of a cheeseburger.
Answer:
Pavlovian

Question:
The only type of currency that flirted with a British spy.
Answer:
Moneypenny

Question:
It happens when a professor's brain goes missing.
Answer:
Absent

Question:
Tax rates and oil prices occasionally take these nature strolls.
Answer:

Question:
It describes an era in history during which lights was hard to come by.
Answer:
Dark Ages

Question:
It is known as the best real estate for toys.
Answer:
Dollhouse

Question:
During the 1800's these turned women into hourglasses and is becoming more popular again these days.
Answer:
Corset

Question:
They are dark-colored creature serenaded by Lennon and McCartney.
Answer:
Blackbird

Question:
Tiny as they are, but they eat homes from the inside out.
Answer:
Termite

Question:
Paul's height is six feet, he's an assistant at a butcher's shop, and wears

size 9 shoes. What does he weight?
Answer:
Meat

Question:
If you can spot one of these eastern warriors, it means they're not doing their job right.
Answer:
Ninja

Question:
It is a standard dimension for both sandwiches and rulers.
Answer:
Footlong

Question:
It is hot tempered and sometimes it blows its top, thus making a mess of everything.
Answer:
Volcano

Question:
Known to be accessorized with feathers, trumpets and harps.
Answer:
Angel

Question:
It is the time in your life when you simultaneously know everything and nothing at an instance.
Answer:

Question:
Not only humans have two that shrink in the light and expand in the dark.
Answer:
Pupil

Question:
It is a path of cow juice spread across the sky but cannot be seen by the naked eye.
Answer:
Milky Way

Question:
Both the original 49ers and opportunistic women share this nickname.
Answer:
Gold Digger

Question:
If it has a quart capacity, how many pennies can you put into a empty piggy bank?
Answer:
One

Question:
The group of animals which hang out in the mist.
Answer:
Gorillas

Question:

433
It stands on one leg with its heart in its head.
Answer:
Cabbage

Question:
Where do fish keep their money?
Answer:
Riverbank

Question:
It is where kings, queens, knights and bishops go to war together.
Answer:
Chess

Question:
Whose big belly supposedly has the ability to dispense good fortune?
Answer:
Buddha

Question:
This could make wooden boy's noses grow.
Answer:
Fib

Question:
It is a form of mechanism invented so you can discover who is following you.
Answer:
Rearview

Question:
If you happen to wear one of these warm garments around, you might get doused in red paint.
Answer:
Fur Coat

Question:
What is probably the most famous dinner party in history?
Answer:
Last Supper

Question:
It is an arctic double breasted formal wear.
Answer:
Snowsuit

Question:
He is not the skinniest of felines.
Answer:
Fat Cat

Question:
It has 4 lucky leaves. What is it?
Answer:
Shamrock

Question:
What is the surname of the pilot of the millennium falcon?
Answer:
Solo

435

Question:
What is greater than god, but more evil than the devil? The rich need it, but the poor already have it. If you eat it, you will die.
Answer:
Nothing

Question:
Poke your fingers in my eyes and I will open wide my jaws. Linen, cloth, quills or paper, my greedy lust devours them all. What am I?
Answer:
Scissors

CONCLUSION

Congratulations you have gone through these riddles, but that's not all. You can still go over them again for your kids to get used to them. I am sure you loved these Question And Answe (especially the ones that made you laugh). You can check for other books by Jimmy Elliott, and continue sharing the bond with your kids.